PAUL,

THE
MAN
WHO
BUILT
BOXES

and other stories

I HOPE YOU ENJOY MEETING THESE CHARACTERS!

FRANK TAVARES

FRANK

BACON PRESS BOOKS
WASHINGTON, DC

2013

The following stories in this collection previously appeared in the publications noted: "My First Ex-wife's Third Wedding," "The Illustrated Sally," "Why Jimmy Mendoza Hated the Late Tamale Jones," "Girl in a Box," and "When It's Over" in *Louisiana Literature: A Review of Literature and the Humanities*; "The Neighbors" in *Story Quarterly*; "The Man Who Built Boxes" in *GW Review: A Literary Journal*; "Max Ryland Meets the Devil" in *Tales of the Talisman*; "Woman with a Gun" in *Connecticut Review*; and "Doin' the Laundry" in *The Writers Post Journal*.

Published in the United States by Bacon Press Books, Washington, DC
www.baconpressbooks.com

Editor and Copyeditor: Lorraine Fico-White
www.magnificomanuscripts.com

Cover Design: Alan Pranke
www.amp13.com

Book Layout and Design: Lorie DeWorken
www.mindthemargins.com

Cover Photo: Asif Akbar

Author Photo: Richard Glinka

ISBN: 978-0-9888779-5-5

Library of Congress Control Number: 2013912804

PRINTED IN THE UNITED STATES OF AMERICA

For the late Leo Connellan, who had faith in my writing before I did

CONTENTS

◻   ◻   ◻

THE MAN WHO BUILT BOXES
and other stories

MY FIRST EX-WIFE'S THIRD WEDDING

"You know," my first ex-wife said, "it never occurred to me that I'd be married three times."

It was a month before her June wedding, and she was triple guessing herself.

"Don't get me wrong, Kenny," she said. "He's a great guy. I haven't felt like this since, well . . ." I could hear the smile in her voice. "Well, since you and I were getting married."

"There's your warning," I said.

Rox had called me from the road. She was somewhere in Ohio behind the wheel of a rental car halfway between an airport and a hotel.

"We were young," she said. "We didn't know what we needed to make it past those first few years."

"Mileage," I said.

"Yes," she said. "Mileage is a good thing. It shows you the landscape."

We'd had parts of this conversation before, although the roles had been reversed. I had been the one planning on getting married a third time.

"And therapy," I said.

"And therapy," she echoed. "That gives you a map."

She paused. I listened to the Boston traffic outside my advertising agency window. It was afternoon rush hour and the frustrations of tired drivers trying to head home were audible.

"Will you come?" she asked.

"To the wedding?"

"Yes. Haven't you been listening?"

"Yes, I've been listening."

"So, will you?"

"I don't know, Rox. Shouldn't you run this past Ed?"

"Ed will want what I want," she said, then laughed. "He's too smitten to object."

"How many people will be there?"

"Just a handful."

"Will Jill?"

She paused again. "Yes, Jill will be there."

I took a deep breath. "I don't know, Rox. I need to think about it."

"You and Jill have been divorced ten years," she said.

"So, you and I have been divorced twenty. What's your point?"

"So, get over it!"

There's an extra level of challenge in arguing with an ex. Especially one who has emerged from the sandstorms of divorce as a friend.

"There's nothing to get over," I said. "She's just not someone I care to be around."

"For a couple of hours you can fake it," Rox said. "My exit's coming up. Be a sport. Just come." She disconnected.

I put down the phone and laid my head on the one bare space on my overflowing desk. The glass was cool on my forehead.

Of course I would go.

The wedding was taking place in a small art gallery outside of Phoenix. Rox had always been partial to southwestern art. Five years before, she had moved from New York to Arizona to enjoy the open sky. "I can work from anywhere," she had said. "All I need is a laptop, a cell phone, and an airport."

Rox was in training and development, a job whose description easily morphed to meet the needs of different clients, and for which she could charge inordinate amounts of money. So much so, that when she divorced her second husband, there was no argument that she would pay the alimony.

I had come into Phoenix the afternoon before the wedding. My hotel was only a mile from the gallery, but the directions to the venue were confusing and I was making a practice run. After several wrong turns, I found the place, an adobe-faced building constructed to resemble an early Spanish mission. The door was an elaborately carved hardwood panel. It was heavy and not particularly inviting as the entrance to a commercial establishment. The gallery itself was larger than I had expected. It was divided into multiple spaces featuring a collection of Native American and Central and South American artifacts, as well as an unexpected focus on Harley Davidson. One inner room featured two Harley hogs on raised platforms across from each other. Each was heavily customized.

"The owner of the gallery is a fabricator," someone with a British accent said behind me.

I turned. For a moment I didn't recognize the woman; forties, black permed hair. It wasn't until she removed her sunglasses and I saw the green eyes . . .

"Jill?"

"Hello, Kenneth," she said.

"I didn't recognize you," I said, feeling a tightening in my lungs.

"Oh, come on," she said, her accent softening the edges of the words. "It hasn't been that long." She held out her left hand for me to take. I'd always hated that left-hand thing. She gave me a kiss on the cheek.

"You look different," I said, trying to reclaim my hand.

"It's the hair," she said, tossing her head. "Do you like it? The blond got to be so boring. Notice anything else?" She stood back, hands on hips, posing.

I hated these tests. "You've been working out," I ventured.

"Oh, Kenneth." She shook her head. "Observation was never your strong suit."

I was beginning to feel that neither was coming to Phoenix.

"It's the boobs," she said. "The boobs."

There is something odd about staring at your ex-wife's breasts.

"I had a little enhancement work."

"Very nice," I managed.

"Thank you."

"Oh, there you are." A man stepped to Jill's side. "Showin' off your new tits?" He had a southwestern accent. Oklahoma, perhaps, or Texas. "Hi," he said, proffering a hand. "Bob Daily." It was a strong handshake.

"This is Kenneth, dear," Jill said before I could introduce myself.

"Well, Kenny!" he said. "Heard a lot about you."

"Hope some of it was good." I'd think of the perfect line later.

Bob was older than Jill by a good fifteen or twenty years. A little shorter than she, about five-six or seven. But there was a pugnacious confidence that spoke of success and money.

"Robert and I are engaged," Jill said.

"Engaged in what?" Bob said with a laugh.

Jill raised her eyebrows. She'd heard that joke before.

"Well, congratulations," I said. "That's wonderful news."

"Thank you, boy." Bob slipped his arm around her waist. "She's a lucky gal."

"Yes, she is."

"Have you seen Roxanne?" Jill asked me. "She was going to meet me here so we could oversee the setup for tomorrow."

"No," I said. "I just got in a little while ago and swung by to make sure I could find the place. Didn't know anyone would be here."

"You haven't planned many weddings, have you," Jill said, then added, "Even your own, as I recall. Of course we'd be here. The ceremony's tomorrow morning."

"Ten o'clock," I said.

Jill smiled. "That's right. You'll be on time, won't you?"

"Yes, I'll be on time."

"Jill hates anyone bein' late 'ceptin' her," Bob said and chuckled. "But, you know that."

"Yes," Jill said with a patient breath as she wiped her lipstick off my cheek with her thumb. "He knows that."

I remembered waiting for her once outside a Boston concert hall. The performance was at eight. She pulled up in a taxi at twenty past. No apology, no explanation. Just an irritation with my irritation. I wondered if chuckling Bob knew how much these charming little idiosyncrasies would be the death of him.

"You ever ride a hog?" Bob asked in response to my silent question. "One a them." He gestured toward the Harleys on display. They were beautiful bikes. Works of art with highly polished chrome and steel.

"Only once," I said.

"I've had a couple," he said, eyes squinting. "Dangerous critters if you don't know what you're doin'. Lotsa idiosyncrasies. The older models can be a little demandin'. But the more you ride 'em, the easier they get to control." He smiled and nodded. "Jill here says she'll buy me a new one for a weddin' present."

I couldn't quite picture her on the back of a Harley.

"Why don't you join us for dinner?" Jill asked.

"Thanks. But I'm exhausted from the trip. Was looking forward to crashing early."

"Don't be a silly," she said. "We won't keep you up late."

They were staying at the same hotel, so I compromised with the promise of an early drink at the bar and managed to excuse myself. As I was crossing the gallery parking lot, I saw Rox. She was getting out of her car. Although we talked often, I hadn't seen her since Jill and I had first gotten divorced. Rox had flown up to Boston for the day to cheer me up, taking me to a movie and buying me dinner.

"Hi, Rox."

She turned and smiled a broad smile that cut across the decade. She looked terrific—fit and tan. The shoulder-length blond hair she used to wear was shorter and its natural auburn. It framed her face.

"Oh, Kenny. I'm so glad you came." She gave me a long hug, then pushed me out to arm's length. "Let's see. Appropriate smile lines, only a couple of gray hairs, same brown eyes. You're holding up pretty well."

"You too."

"That's life in Phoenix," she said. "Although I'm not as careful about the sun as I should be. By the time I'm fifty I'll be really weathered, but it sure beats the hell out of those New York winters."

"You should have moved years ago."

"Easy to say."

A tall man got out of the passenger side of her car. Athletic. Late-forties, early fifties. A tennis player. I could tell by the arms. And the shoes.

"Kenny, this is Ed. My betrothed."

"Oh, Ken," he said, shaking hands. "I've heard a lot about you."

"I hope some of it was good." I didn't have the new line yet.

"Actually, I'm hoping that Rox'll talk as nicely about me as she does about you if this doesn't work out."

"Doesn't work out?" Rox swatted him on the arm. "Doesn't work out? What are you doing? Planning ahead?"

They laughed.

"I'm meeting Jill here," Rox said. "Want to pop in for a minute, say hi? Get it over with?"

"I just saw her. Met Bob."

Rox smiled. "See, it wasn't so bad."

"Made me promise to have a drink with them later."

"We'll join you," Rox volunteered a rescue.

I glanced at Ed. He nodded.

It was a little after five when I headed down to the bar. The two couples were already sitting around a table nibbling bar nuts. Rox was the first to see me. She waved.

"Lotsa folk don't think there's that much difference in how they mate," Bob was saying. "But if you look at the couplings, that's the proof."

"Should I come back later?" I asked.

Ed smiled, Jill looked bored, and Rox gestured for me to sit next to her.

"Hose couplings," Bob said. "Ah'm in the hose bidniss."

"Garden hoses?" I asked.

"No, son," Bob chuckled. "Engineerin' hoses. Everythin' from aircraft engines to those Harleys we saw today. Even got hoses on the space shuttle. High-end specialty stuff. Got a little plant down near Waco, one in Mexico, and one opening in Vietnam." He pronounced the latter as if it rhymed with "beet ma'am."

"Robert is the Hose King," Jill said, her beautiful accent giving the title a true rise to royalty.

"And pretty soon, you'll be ma Hose Queen," he said with another chuckle.

The waitress appeared. "Manchester!" she said, looking at Jill.

"I beg your pardon," my second ex-wife said.

"You're from Manchester." The waitress, whose nametag said Margaret, had an accent similar to hers, just a tad less cultivated.

"Originally," Jill said. "I was born there."

"Me too," the waitress said. "We're certainly a long way from home."

"You've noticed," Jill said.

We ordered our drinks. Bob finished up about the hoses. There's a lot more to hoses than I'd thought.

Ed asked me if the advertising business was as glamorous as it looked on TV. I told him it depended on the day, the client, and the caffeine.

"So, Ed, what kind of business are you in?" I asked.

"Real estate," he answered. "Development. Primarily retirement communities, but some commercial."

"All with tennis courts?"

He smiled. "As many as I can muster. Used to play professionally. Like to spread the religion."

"It's how we met," Rox said. "I was playing with a friend and noticed this athlete on the next court, sculpted body glistening with sweat, primal noises emanating with every swing. And this guy she was playing didn't look that bad either."

We laughed at the old joke.

"So where was Ed?" Bob asked.

Rox looked at him.

"Ed," Bob repeated. "You said it's how you met."

"He was the guy on the next court," Rox said.

"Playin' with the sweaty gal."

"Yeah."

"Oh."

Margaret brought our drinks. I held mine above the table. "It's appropriate to offer a toast." My companions raised their glasses. "To Roxanne and Ed." I started to take a sip.

"That's it?" Rox asked. "That's all you're going to say? No wishes for a great new life, or even allusions to this unusual gathering of your exes?" The group laughed. "I don't know, Kenny. This may be your last shot. I'm not planning on doing this again."

"Well, I do wish you both—I wish us all—well. And, Rox, at the risk of taking credit for all of us being here this evening, I'm happy to see you so happy." I raised my glass again. "Here's to Roxanne and Ed. A wonderful new life that's richly deserved."

"Much better," she said.

"Here here," said Bob as we clinked glasses.

Rox and Jill excused themselves for the ladies room.

"It is a bit of an unusual gathering," Ed said. "I feel like Bob and I should be asking you for advice."

"Yeah," said Bob. "Any tips? Don't wanna make the same screw-ups you did."

"Sorry, gentlemen, you're on your own."

By the time the ladies came back, we'd ordered a second round. By the third round, we ordered dinner from the bar menu. Bob had settled back into his chair, content to add sporadic hose comments and to make less than subtle attempts at touching Jill's enhancements. Each time she'd casually move his hand to a more neutral position along her thigh. Ed entertained us with stories of traveling as a professional tennis player and fun tales of construction snafus. I had to admit it was better than watching a movie alone in my room. Jill and a tipsy Bob were the first to leave, Bob sliding his hand from the small of her back to a squeeze of her rear as Jill guided him out of the bar. A few minutes later, Ed excused himself. It was suddenly very quiet.

"Thank you for coming," Rox said. She took my hand. "It sounds funny, but I really wanted to share this with you. And I thought if you didn't come, I just might never see you again." I squeezed her fingers. She put her head on my shoulder.

"So do you think Jill and Bob are as doomed as I do?" she asked.

"Definitely. If they actually get married, I'd give it six months tops."

"Well, if she buys him that Harley and pushes him to ride without a helmet, that may be all the time she needs."

"She'll inherit the hose kingdom."

"Maybe not. He's got adult kids running the 'bidniss.' It may not be as easy as her last one."

"There was one before Bob?" I asked.

"Two," Rox said. "Almost three. Don't you keep up with all your exes?"

"I told you I'm not comfortable having much contact with her."

"You did fine tonight."

"I took your advice," I said. "And faked it."

"Well it worked," she said. "You even fooled me."

We sat quietly, listening to a Muzak rendition of a 1980s disco hit.

"Why didn't you get married last spring?" Rox asked. "After our phone calls, I really thought that's what you wanted."

"I guess I just didn't have enough faith," I said. "Didn't want to chance a third failure. Besides, she wanted kids right away."

"But you've always wanted kids."

"I used to. As I've gotten older, I'm not sure it would be the best idea. By the time they finished high school, I'd be too old to attend graduation."

"You exaggerate."

"Not by much."

"I always thought you'd make a wonderful father." Rox took a deep breath. "It's one of the few things I regret. That we weren't able to have children."

I nodded.

"They'd be out of college by now," she said.

"Maybe," I said. "Ed have kids?"

"Two teenage boys who live with their mom in Albuquerque. They'll stay with us part of each summer and on holidays."

"That'll be a new adventure."

"That it will."

Margaret the waitress stopped by. The bar was getting crowded. "Are you sure there's nothing else I can get for you?" she asked, picking up the empties.

"No," I said. "Thanks."

"I heard you talking about your wedding tomorrow," Margaret said as she lay down the bill. "You're a lovely couple. I really wish you well."

Rox smiled and squeezed my hand. "Thank you. We're going to be very happy."

"I can tell," Margaret said. "You already look as if you've been content with each other for years."

"We have been," Rox said. "We have been."

We split the tab, Rox noting that Bob had slipped away without donating anything, then she walked me to the elevator.

"Funny how time plays tricks," Rox said as the door opened. "Doesn't seem that long ago that we'd be heading to the same room."

"No," I said. "It doesn't."

We hugged longer than Ed might have appreciated, then kissed a quick good night. As the door closed I felt a fleeting pang and raised my hand to wave goodbye. Rox was already halfway across the lobby.

My room felt very empty. I turned on the television, welcoming the voices as I sat on the edge of the bed and took off my shoes. There was a quiet knock on the door. I got up and looked through the peephole. It was Jill. The tightness in my lungs returned.

"Hi, Kenneth," she said as I opened the door. "How about one last drink for old time's sake?" She was holding a champagne bottle and two glasses.

"Well, thanks, but I'm really wiped. Still on eastern time. I need to get some sleep."

"Just one." She smiled. "Just one."

I stepped back and she walked past me, kicking off her shoes. I looked down the hall before closing the door.

"Where's Bob?"

"Oh, he's snoring away. He had one nip too many. Was out as soon as we got back to the room. I didn't even have the pleasure of berating him for being such a boor at dinner. No fun. Very frustrating."

She gave the room the once-over. I was glad my things were neatly stowed. She handed the bottle to me, then set the glasses on the table.

"He seems like a nice guy," I said, unwrapping the foil and working on the wire.

"He is." She flopped into a chair. "But I make a better princess than a queen. I don't have much desire to travel with him to trade shows and entertain customers with feigned enthusiasm about hose couples."

"Couplings," I said and eased out the cork.

"What?"

"Hose couplings, not couples."

"You make my point." She held out her glass.

I filled it, then mine. With a touch, we sipped without a toast.

"It's nice to see you, Kenneth." She tucked her legs under her and leaned back, comfortable on the chair. She was in partial silhouette from the table lamp. "You're the only one who understood me."

If she hadn't said it in such a serious tone, I would have laughed. Instead, I sat opposite her and took another sip.

"I'd forgotten how much I've missed you." She sipped. "Do you ever miss me?"

"I often think about you," I said.

She nodded while she interpreted the remark, then smiled. "Would you like to inspect them?"

"What?"

"My enhancements. Or as The Hose King would so eloquently put it, my 'new tits.'"

"Oh."

"I'd be curious about your reaction, seeing as you knew the originals so well." She gently swirled the champagne in her glass.

"I don't think that would be a good idea," I said. "Besides, that was a very long time ago."

She smiled and with her free hand undid the first button of her blouse. "Ten years, ten minutes. Does it really make any difference?"

I held my glass with both hands and looked at her. "Yes," I said. "It does."

She locked her eyes on mine and undid another button.

"Jill. Don't."

"Ooh," she said, her fingers moving down to the third. "That makes me randy. I always loved it when you were assertive."

I started to chuckle. "No you didn't," I said. "It used to piss you off. You didn't even like me choosing the restaurant."

Jill took a deep breath. I wasn't sure if it was to better display her enhancements or because of frustration that I wasn't following her lead. Her fingers hesitated on the fourth button, then momentarily caressed her exposed cleavage. I kept my eyes on hers. "Oh, Kenneth." She put down her glass. "How many men would love to be sitting right where you are now."

"Jill, that's something I'll never know."

She smiled, took another deep breath, then slowly refastened her buttons. "Perhaps I underestimated you."

"Once or twice."

She sighed, then got up. "I'll leave you the rest of the champagne," she said, refilling her glass.

"That's not necessary," I said, standing.

"I know." She picked up her shoes. "But you'll want a sip or two when you slip into your big, lonely bed tonight and realize what you missed."

"You're very thoughtful."

"Yes. I am. Despite what you might think." She smiled and headed toward the door. I started to open it for her. She turned and gave me a warm kiss. "One touch before I leave?" she dared me.

I put my hand on her right breast and gave it a gentle squeeze. She put her hand over mine and held it tightly against her. Her smiled broadened. "Very nice hands."

"Very nice enhancements."

"Thank you. I knew you'd like them." She gave me a last quick kiss, then opened the door. "Good night, dear Kenneth."

"Good night, Jill."

And she padded down the hall, shoes dangling in one hand, champagne glass high in the other.

A large desert painting on one wall of the gallery provided the visual theme for the wedding. The cacti in the painting were mirrored in the room by a half-dozen life-size saguaro in various mediums. Two were paper-mache. Two others were wood, one carved from a tree foreign to the area. Another was industrial grade cardboard, layers glued together to give it form and substance. The last was metal, fabricated from motorcycle parts. It stood opposite the two customized Harleys.

A second gallery was set up as a champagne bar to host the reception. And tucked into a third, a string quartet provided a cultured ambience that fit surprisingly well into the desert scene. There were about a dozen people. I didn't recognize anyone. A teenaged boy sat in the front. I figured he had to be one of Ed's kids. Rox had said it would be a small wedding with only a few friends. These must be folks she and Ed knew from Phoenix. Jill and I would be the only ones from her past life, an unconventional little family. As for Jill, I didn't see either her or Bob. Jill was probably helping Rox adjust wedding regalia, but I was surprised that Bob wasn't making the rounds.

A tall fellow walked to the front of the room. He wore a big smile and an ill-fitting blue blazer. His brown hair was pulled back in a ponytail. A moment later, Ed followed, dressed in jeans and a blue oxford shirt. No tie. The quartet shifted into the bridal march, and we all stood and turned toward the back.

I tried to remember the last time I had seen Rox in a dress. She'd always preferred casual-jeans or shorts, simple tops. It was a nice surprise to see her walking into the room wearing something else. It wasn't a traditional wedding dress, but an off-white cotton, southwestern in style and Native American in charm. A dress to celebrate a woman's passage.

As Rox made it to the front and the tall man with the ponytail invited us to sit, Jill slipped into the chair next to me.

"Good morning," she whispered. "Sleep well in your big empty bed?" She gave my leg a little squeeze. She was wearing a white blouse that showed cleavage and displayed her lack of need for a bra. Bob sat down next to her. He looked over, gave me a wink, and put his arm around the back of his fiancée's chair.

Jill leaned over. "She looks great, doesn't she?"

I nodded.

The tall man thanked us all for coming to witness the marriage of Roxanne and Edward. The ceremony unfolded nicely. The man's homily was short. He told about meeting them both in this very room when they had visited his gallery. And how they had met each other while admiring the very painting that hung on the wall behind him, a sign that they must be compatible. Then he led them through the vows, parts of which Rox and Ed extemporized.

Ed spoke of finding happiness and stretched a lost-in-the-desert metaphor past the point of elasticity. Rox spoke of her surprise at how life evolves and how events of the past overlap and cross with those of the present. She looked at me when she said she was the sum of all the people she had known and for whom she had cared, then turned to Ed and welcomed him into her life with a promise to love and care for him. Despite myself, my eyes moistened. Jill handed me a tissue. The tall man talked about his vested power, then pronounced them woman and husband, man and wife. We all applauded, Bob the loudest, as they kissed. The quartet struck up a traditional post-ceremony chord as Rox and Ed turned to greet their friends, shaking hands, hugging, kissing cheeks.

"It looks so simple, doesn't it?" Jill said to me. "Something you do every day."

"How many weddings do we have among the three of us?" I asked.

"Nine," she answered without hesitation. "And almost half of them are mine."

Rox and Ed moved toward us, holding hands and beaming. Rox gave Jill a big hug, then turned to me. She held both my hands as she looked in my eyes. Her radiance startled me. I wanted to tell her, but no words came out. She kissed me on both cheeks. Ed followed with a handshake and a silent nod.

As if on cue, we all moved toward the adjoining gallery. Bob struck up a conversation with a fellow who had been admiring the Harleys. Jill stood dutifully by while Bob pointed out a hose near the carburetor. The tall man was standing near a painting with a guest who was trying to explain what he thought the artist had meant. Rox and Ed were passing out glasses of champagne, and the quartet had settled into the background ambience.

I slipped out the door and headed toward my rental car. In the parking lot, the teenaged boy from inside was decorating an upscale SUV with signs of the newly married. The sky was clear. The sun was hot. It was a beautiful day. I drove toward the airport. Without warning, a wave of melancholy washed over me. It left me breathless as I realized I would probably never see Rox—or Jill—again. In a moment, it subsided. I took a deep breath. Rox was right. We are the sum of all who have been in our lives.

Two hours later, I looked down on the city as my plane climbed into the sky. I imagined Rox and Jill looking up and waving. It had been a remarkable visit, past lives and paths crossing with the present. But it had only been a visit. I turned forward in my seat as my two ex-wives receded into the distance.

THE ILLUSTRATED SALLY

Twenty-nine-year-old Sally Quantico walked away from her job at noon. She hadn't planned it, but it seemed the right thing to do. She didn't tell anyone. She just left at the lunch break and kept on going. Past the office and the time clock, past the security booth in the parking lot, past the coffee truck on the street outside the gate, and past the bus stop at the end of the block. She walked home, all four miles of it. Walked her five-foot-four, tattooed, dirty-blond self with a sense of purpose, although she wasn't quite sure yet what the purpose might be.

The apartment was empty, just as she'd found it the afternoon before. Robbie had taken the furniture. Even the broken secretary desk she'd rescued from the alley behind the Chinese restaurant. He'd left her the clothes that were hanging in the bedroom closet. The ones from the dresser were in a pile by the window. The mattress with a sheet was on the floor. In the bathroom, her toiletries had been rifled, but most were there. Toothbrush, the makeup she used to soften the inch-long scar on her jaw, and her prescription meds.

He hadn't found the money; nearly eight thousand dollars she'd hidden in an envelope behind the toilet. He would have grabbed it if he knew it was there. It had taken her more than a year to pull it together. Five dollars here, ten there, and six thousand she'd won off a scratch lottery card she'd never told him about. She almost did tell him once. He'd gotten canned for coldcocking his boss after an argument about overtime. Laid him out in front of the crew. Someone called the cops and Robbie found himself facing an assault charge. He had no money for bail. She went to the courthouse the following day with the envelope, but the charges were dropped before she had to give up the secret.

He was a deadbeat. She'd known that from the first time they ate in a real restaurant. It was an Italian place. It wasn't that he'd stuck her with the check, it was that he didn't look at it before slapping down a credit card. No concern for the money. And when she moved in with him, she learned he had a pocket full of plastic, most maxed out and everything past due. While he was out of work, she paid his rent and learned from an irate landlady that it was two months late.

She wondered who helped him empty the apartment so quickly. They must have started as soon as she'd left for work the morning before, throwing things into boxes, carrying stuff down the stairs. She thought he'd been asleep when she'd showered and dressed. He'd come in late the night before. She didn't know what time but was glad he didn't wake her. He'd slipped beneath the covers and kept to his side of the bed. In the morning when she left, he was still facing the edge, no body parts straying into the center no-man's-land.

She'd expected something to happen, but not this. When she discovered the empty apartment the previous day, she was stunned. She had looked for a note. Some final words. Even a "Dear Sally, Fuck you" scrawled on the back of some envelope. But he'd left nothing. When her vision blurred, she'd sat cross-legged on the bare living room floor with a cigarette to calm herself. It was her first that week.

Dinner that night was Chinese from across the street. She ate from the box and washed down her evening meds with a beer from the neighborhood convenience store. She was tired as if she hadn't slept for days, and her head ached. She took a shower and crawled onto the mattress. Just seconds after she pulled up the sheet, she was asleep. Shortly after dawn, she had raced through her morning routine—bathroom, teeth, meds, dress—and headed out the door before much could register. It wasn't until she transferred buses near the high school that she felt adrift. But by the time she clocked in at the plant, she had it under control. At least until the lunch break.

Returning to the empty apartment wasn't as unsettling as she had feared. This time she actually felt some relief. It wasn't as if he had done anything she hadn't contemplated herself; picking up and leaving, just getting the hell out, not looking back. There was one big difference between them, though. She would have taken nothing. She would have left everything behind.

Her cell phone vibrated. She looked at the ID and wavered before answering.

"Hi, Kathy."

"Sally, where are you?" asked the woman. "I didn't see you in the caf at lunch. And you're not at your machine. You okay?"

"Yeah, I'm fine."

"What's going on?"

"Robbie left."

Kathy hesitated, then said, "Well, fuck 'im. He was an asshole."

"Still is."

"Sweetie, I'll call you when I get off. You want me to bring you anything?"

"No, don't bother," said Sally. "I've got everything I need."

☐ ☐ ☐

The bus was late. Sally walked back into the Union Station waiting room and looked for an update.

"Twenty minutes," the agent told her.

She lowered her backpack onto a bench and sat down. She was warm and took off her jacket. The intercity buses shared the station with AMTRAK and commuter rail. The building was a large and busy place built in the 1920s, one of the dozens that shared its name with others around the country. It was frantic this late afternoon with commuters returning from New York. The bus waiting area was tucked in a corner at one end of the building. Sally had thought about taking the train into the city and then switching over to Greyhound. But it wouldn't be worth the few minutes she'd save, and she'd have the hassle of getting from Grand Central over to the Port Authority. Besides, the bus was a little cheaper and she needed to stretch her money as long as possible; she didn't know when she'd be able to add to it.

Chicago. That's what she'd decided. She would go to Chicago. It would take a day and a half, but she didn't mind. She liked to travel. Gave her time to think. She hadn't been to the windy city in a dozen years. Not since she left a note on her mother's kitchen table saying she had had enough. She doubted anyone would remember her. She didn't even know if her parents still lived there. She'd look for a job and have a chance to start over again. Chicago, San Diego,

Austin, New Haven. She'd lived on her own in all four corners of the country. And lived in a handful of other places before that. Military bases, mostly. Her father, a marine-lifer, dragged them all over. But it was Chicago she remembered the clearest. It would be full circle.

Kathy had called after work as promised. "You sure you don't want me to come over?"

"I'm fine," Sally said. "Really. I'm just gonna take a little time off. I'll call you next week." It was a lie.

Sally counted the people waiting. There was a mom with three kids under the age of five, and an older gay couple with a suitcase and a shopping bag. By the door, a heavy woman stood with a cane that seemed more for style and protection than mobility, and a thirty-something fellow with a shaved head wearing a wool coat despite the mild fall evening. He looked uncomfortable with his hands in the pockets. He was also talking to himself. Sally looked for a Bluetooth, but there wasn't any. She turned away when he caught her.

There were plenty of empties on the bus. Sally sat next to a window halfway back on the driver's side. The man with the coat chose the seat across the aisle.

The bus started to move, rocking over the curb as it pulled onto the street. Sally reclined her seatback the few inches she could and closed her eyes.

"Nice sleeve," said the man.

Sally glanced over. He was leaning toward her.

"Took a lot of time," he said. He was pointing at the tattoos that ran down her arm to just above the wrist. It was a chain of flowers and vines with a handful of faces hidden in the leaves, among them, renditions of the drama masks of tragedy and comedy.

"I like the necklace, too," he said. "That one took a few visits."

"Yeah," Sally said as she shifted in her seat.

"Local?"

She looked at him.

"The work," he said. "The art. Done here?"

"Some."

"I like the masks. You act?"

"No, I don't act," she said. "Look, I've had a real bad day. I'm sorry if I'm not too sociable."

"Apology accepted," he said.

Sally turned away.

"My name's Jake," he said. "I'm an actor."

She ignored him.

"I saw you watching me at the station," he said. "I'm not a nut case. I was running lines for a play. I probably shouldn't do that in public."

Sally took a deep breath. "No, you shouldn't." She turned away from the window. "So does this actor thing explain the coat? Part of some costume?"

"Sort of," he said.

The bus stopped for a light, then pulled onto the entry ramp for the highway.

"You might want to rethink that too," she said.

"Actually," Jake said, "there's another reason I wear the coat. It's to keep Little Jake warm."

"Oh, Jesus," Sally said, grabbing her pack. "That's all I need." She stood up. "Some goddamned pervert with pet names for his body parts."

"No," Jake said, gesturing for her to sit down. "It's not what you think." He reached in his pocket and pulled out a small animal.

Sally stepped back, raising a hand in front of her.

"Little Jake. My ferret."

The rodent looked at Sally and sniffed the air between them. Before she could say anything, Jake stuffed him back in the pocket. "The lining's loose," he said. "He likes roaming around in it."

Sally didn't sit, but shook her head. "You really are a whack job."

"Please," said Jake. "Stay. No more surprises."

Sally sat, but with her pack in her lap, ready to move in an instant.

"I admit it's a little weird," he said. "But I've had him for a while. Can't just leave him when I travel."

"So, if you're an actor," Sally said, "what's this play you're practicing?"

"*Marat Sade.*" He smiled. "Full title, *The Persecution and Assassination of Jean-Paul Marat as Performed by the Inmates of the Asylum of Charenton Under the Direction of the Marquis de Sade.*"

"That doesn't help your case," she said.

"I take it you've never heard of it."

"I'm not a big theater fan."

"Then why the drama masks?"

Sally looked at her arm. "Because life is full of drama."

Jake nodded. "So, what was it? Childhood trauma? Old boyfriend?"

"I don't see that's any of your business," she said.

Jake nodded again. "Sorry."

The bus braked. Sally braced herself against the seat in front of her. They picked up speed again. Jake took a sandwich out of a bag.

"I have a theory about tattoos," he said.

Sally didn't rise to the bait. Little Jake scurried in the coat lining over big Jake's knee. Jake nudged him upward through the cloth. The ferret stuck its head out of the pocket. Jake pulled a piece of bread off the sandwich and fed it to him.

"Tattoos are always covering up something." Little Jake crawled farther out. "Always hiding something." Jake gave him another piece of the sandwich.

"So you're a shrink, too," Sally said.

"Actors analyze," he said. "It's how we find the character in a role. Your tattoos are interesting. Lots of faces in the leaves. What's that about?"

"You know something, Jake? Fuck off."

Sally thought she'd lost him at the Port Authority. Before their bus came to a stop, she'd grabbed her pack and scooted up the aisle putting the mother with three kids between them. By the time he'd managed to exit, Sally was not in his line of sight. From behind an advertising display, she watched him looking for her, and relaxed when he headed out of the building.

She had a couple of hours before the Chicago bus. In the ladies room, she looked tired in the mirror, and her scar was angry. She dabbed on a little concealer to soften it, then found a place to eat where she washed down her evening meds with a Diet Coke. She bought a paperback and hid herself in it while she waited for the departure announcement. She was among the first to board after the gate opened. Unlike the last coach, this one would have fewer free seats. She sat on the left side by the window and set the pack next to her, hoping no one would ask her to move it. She closed her eyes and feigned sleep, listening to the other passengers settling in.

"This seat taken?"

She looked up. It was Jake. People were behind him waiting for her answer. Reluctantly, she lifted the pack.

"I can put that up for you," he said.

She answered by placing it on her lap. He put his bag on the rack, then sat.

"Full bus," he said.

"What are you doing here?"

"Same as you."

"You're going to Chicago."

"Yeah."

"Long trip for your little friend."

"He's okay as long as I feed him and walk him every couple of hours. Likes to sleep."

The bus backed out of its slot.

"Okay, Mr. Actor Shrink, why the fuck you stalking me?"

"I'm not stalking you."

"So it's just a coincidence you end up sitting here?"

Jake leaned his head back against the seat. "Not entirely," he answered. "It's your ink." He pulled up the sleeves of his coat. Both arms were covered with tattoos. On one a small gallery of animals including a classic tiger and a not-so-classic ferret. On the other, a paragraph in elegant font with a portrait of Shakespeare at the bottom.

"*Hamlet*," Jake said. "Act 3, Scene 1. Polonius's advice to his son Laertes."

Sally looked at the designs as he rotated his arms. "So," she said. "Now we supposed to be special pals?"

Jake smiled. "Yeah, sort of."

Sally leaned back and crossed her arms on the top of her pack. "Look, we're not pals," she said. "And I'd appreciate it if you and your little friend just let me the hell alone."

Jake nodded. "I'm visiting a buddy in Chicago."

Sally shook her head. "What part of 'let me the hell alone' don't you understand?"

"That's the real reason I'm on this bus," he said. "My friend's in the hospital. Probably not going to make it through the weekend."

Sally took a long breath. "Sorry about that."

"Thanks."

She pulled out her book and read for a while. It was a memoir by a well-known television journalist second guessing what she'd given up to chase her career. Only after Jake was asleep, did Sally close her eyes.

It was a little after 2:00 a.m. when they stopped someplace in Pennsylvania. Sally woke to find Jake studying the illustrations on her arm.

"Sorry," he said when she caught him.

They had thirty minutes. Jake disappeared with his little friend. Sally had a cigarette, freshened up, had a second cigarette, and reboarded. She caught Jake flipping through her paperback and wondered if he'd been snooping in her pack. She lifted it onto the rack before she sat down.

"I hate riding the bus," he said.

"Well, don't let me stop you if you want to get off and hitchhike."

"How come all the faces are upside down?" he asked.

Sally looked at him.

"On your arm," he said and pointed at several of the portraits.

She held out her arm and turned it. "So I can see them," she said.

Jake stared at the pictures. "They're all looking away."

"Yeah," said Sally. "None of them dare look me in the eye."

"People you know?"

"People I knew. They remind me of things not to do again."

The driver did a count and started the bus toward the highway. They hadn't traveled more than a hundred yards when there was a scream from the back, followed by a second, then a third.

"It's a rat!" someone yelled, and pandemonium broke out. People in the aisles, people pulling their feet onto seats, shouts and curses. The driver turned on the cabin lights and stopped.

"Oh jeez," said Jake, patting down his coat. "It's Little Jake." He tried to stand in the aisle. "It's not a rat," he shouted over the noise. "It's a ferret! It's my pet ferret! Don't hurt him! Where is he? I'll get him."

It took a minute for Jake to find the animal. It was scurrying in a panic underfoot, trying to escape the chaos. By the time Little Jake was rescued, the driver was wading back through the passengers, a number of whom were yelling and cursing at Jake.

The driver calmed them, then turned to Jake. "You can't have animals in here, man," he said. "What are you thinking? I can't have some rat running around the coach."

"It's not a rat," Jake said as he protected Little Jake in his hands.

"I don't care what that thing is, either it gets off or you both get off."

"He's my pet," said Jake. "I can't just turn him loose."

"Then you need to get off this bus. You understand?"

Sally had been glad to see him go. She'd have the seat to herself and no one snooping in her stuff. He had grabbed his pack from the rack and made his way down the aisle to the unkind comments of their fellow passengers.

"So why'd you get off after me?" Jake asked.

Sally was sitting across from him at a rest stop table. She took a sip of coffee. "You looked so pitiful carrying that little rat out into the night. Wanted to see how the melodrama played out."

"It's a ferret," he said and looked at his watch.

"Where's your friend coming from?" Sally asked.

"An hour or so south."

"What's he do?"

"Teaches at one of the state universities."

"Theater?"

Jake smiled. "Physics, actually."

"Gotta be a good friend to haul his ass out of bed at three in the morning."

"We go back a ways. We've rescued each other a few times."

"And it's his turn?"

In the cold light of the rest stop, needing a shave, and needing sleep, Jake looked older to Sally than he did when she first saw him at the beginning of the journey.

"You visiting someone in Chicago?" he asked.

Sally took another sip of coffee. "Not exactly," she said.

"Work? Home?"

"Moving there."

Jake nodded. "You're traveling light."

"Got what I need."

It was slow in the rest stop. The overnight crew was cleaning. One worker was mopping the floor in wide arcs and rinsing the dirt into a wheeled bucket. Another was wiping down displays in the souvenir shop. Those behind the food counter were restocking after the rush with the bus and trying to entertain each other. It was slow, but the activity was steady, punctuated by tired drivers who filtered in from the interstate.

"You never told me your name," said Jake.

"Sally."

Jake reached his hand over the table. She took it. "Glad to meet you, Sally. Got a last name?"

"What's yours?" she asked.

"Holland," he said

"Like tulips."

He smiled as if he'd never heard the line before.

"Quantico," said Sally.

"Like that marine base in Virginia," he said.

Sally smiled, surprised he'd pegged it.

The plan was to rent a car and drive the rest of the way. Jake's friend would take them to Harrisburg where they'd pick up a rental at the airport. Jake would pay for it, and Sally would help with the driving. When they got to the city, he'd drop her wherever she wanted.

Little Jake rustled in the coat lining. Jake looked around and stuffed a piece of roll into his pocket. "You been to Chicago before?" Jake asked.

"Lived there once," she said. "But it's been a while."

"How long?"

"High school."

"Left for college?"

She laughed. "Not exactly. I ran off with a guy my junior year. My family was pretty fucked up, and it was the easiest way out."

"And how'd that work out for you?

"Predictably. He was a trucker. I lived on the road with him for a month before he dumped me in San Diego."

"Well, if you're going to be stranded, I guess there are worse places."

"I thought that, too."

"He in your gallery?"

She pointed inside her forearm. The face was heavy with a Fu Manchu mustache.

"Smooth talker," she said as if she'd heard Jake ask how she could have been attracted to him. "And I was fifteen."

"What'd you do in San Diego?"

"Lied about my age. Got a waitress job. Learned a little Spanish."

Jake took the opening Sally had given him. "How about that guy?" he asked, touching a portrait below the first. The face was gaunt, the hair long.

"Musician," she said. "Rock and roll. Drummer." She wrapped her hands around the cup. "My groupie year. Lived on a tour bus most of the time, an occasional motel. Knew the tour was over when they left me asleep backstage after a gig in Austin. They loaded up, got on the bus, and drove off."

"Ouch."

"I liked Austin, though," she said. "Easy place to live. Stayed for a couple of years."

"Doing what?"

"Different things. Worked in a bar. Then a clothing store. Even got a job for a while in physical therapy." She made little quotes with her fingers.

She was afraid he'd ask what she meant exactly by "physical therapy," but instead Jake sipped his coffee.

"Why'd you leave?" he said.

Sally shrugged. "Was a velvet trap. The kind of place I could wake up in one day and realize I'd spent my whole life there."

"And you weren't afraid to pick up and start over again someplace else?"

"I've always been pretty lucky finding work," Sally said. "Even had a couple of jobs that came with health insurance." She sipped her coffee. "That's how I found out I'm dying."

Jake's friend Bartosz, "Call me Bart," was a flirtatious guy. He insisted that Sally sit in the front where he could regale her with stories of how he and Jake partied their way through grad school, and where he could punctuate the tales by touching her thigh, occasionally letting his hand rest for a moment or two before giving it a squeeze, each time a little farther up her leg.

"I always got the pretty ones," Bart said, his eastern European accent just exotic enough to excuse some of his social ineptitude. "That's why I don't know how you're with him instead of me."

"First of all," said Sally, "I'm not 'with him.' It's a coincidence that we're going to the same place."

"But you got off the bus," said Bart. "That means something. You could have stayed on the bus, but you got off. Why did you get off?"

"It was a mistake," said Sally, lifting his hand off her leg.

"Hey, Bart," said Jake from the back. "How's Edie doing?"

Bart cleared his throat. "She's fine."

"Edie is Bart's wife," said Jake. "They've been together for quite a while. Tell Sally about your family, Bart, your two girls."

Bart looked at Jake in the mirror. "I have two daughters," he said.

"And how old are they now?" asked Jake.

"Five and seven."

"They're beautiful," said Jake. "Just like their mother. You're a lucky guy, Bart."

Bart nodded. "Yes. I am."

At the airport, Bart insisted on coming in with them. While Jake was at the rental counter, Bart pulled Sally aside. He stood too close when he said, "Let me drive you to Chicago."

"Thanks, but it'll be easier with the rental car."

"I don't mean with Jake," he said. "You and me. Jake won't mind. He and I go back a long time."

"What about your wife?" Sally asked.

"What about her?" he said. "She's not here. Come on. While Jake's arguing with that clerk. It'll be a big joke on him. We can call him from the road. Make him jealous. We'll have some fun. Maybe stop a few times to get to know each other." He reached up and traced the scar on her face.

Sally grabbed his wrist. "Bart, you like anal?"

He smiled. "Sure. Who doesn't."

"Me for one," she said. "You're an asshole, Bart, and I don't fuck assholes." She threw his hand off and started back to the counter.

"But," he said grabbing her arm, "you'll fuck him for a free ride."

Sally swung around and clocked him. She punched him full force closed fist in the face. He staggered backward, then fell on his rear, blood spurting from his nose. Jake turned just in time to see Bart fall. He ran over.

"Jeez! What happened?"

"Why don't you ask him?" Sally said, swinging her pack onto her shoulder. "I'm sure he'll have a good story. Jake, nice meeting you, but I'm outta here." Before he could say anything, she headed toward the escalator. She looked back once to make sure neither of them was following. Bart was trying to staunch the bleeding. Jake was trying to help but looked torn, as he watched Sally disappear up the moving stairs.

She found a restroom. It was empty. She hid herself in a stall. She hung her backpack on the hook and sat. She felt it far back in her head, a steady throbbing matched to the rhythm of her pulse. It didn't hurt much yet, but she knew it would. Maybe her morning meds would stave it off one more time. If only she could reach inside the back of her scalp. Reach the back of her brain. Squeeze it, push it aside. Reach past it and pluck out the tumor. Pull it out. Throw it on the floor. Step on it. Flatten it. Kill it and flush it down the toilet.

She put her palm on her forehead, then both hands on her cheeks. She was sweating. She closed her eyes and started to cry. She sobbed, letting the tears track down her face.

Someone knocked on the door. "Everything okay in there?"

"Yeah," Sally said. "I'm fine. Period starting. Cramps."

"Say no more," the voice replied as it faded behind a door at the end of the row.

Sally waited for the woman to leave before she came out. Her eyes were red. She splashed water on her face. Back in the concourse, she took the handful of pills that were helping her buy time. They couldn't cure it, but they could push back against some of the symptoms. How long did she have? Six months? A year? That was optimistic. She knew the prognosis.

And so had Robbie.

□   □   □

"I'm sorry," he said.

He was standing behind her as she sat watching television. He leaned over and kissed her neck, then slid his hand over her shoulder to her breast. His other hand moved past her stomach to inside her thighs.

"Why didn't you say goodbye?"

"Because I'm a fuckin' prick. You knew that. That's what you liked about me. My fuckin' prick." Robbie laughed. "Hey," he asked as he squeezed her breast. "Do I get my own tattoo?"

Sally jolted awake. She couldn't tell where she was. Her vision was blurred and the sound was muffled. She blinked and rubbed her eyes. It took a moment before the airport waiting area came into focus. It was busier than when she first sat down. She looked at the clock. Still an hour before her flight.

"Good morning," someone said behind her. She turned. Jake was sitting there.

Reflexively she grabbed for her pack.

"Wait," he said.

"Now you *are* stalking me," she said.

"No, I'm not. I just wanted to apologize for my friend and make sure you were all right."

"How'd you get past TSA?"

"Bought a ticket."

"Like I said. Stalking."

"No," he said. "If I was stalking you, I'd be on the same flight. Mine's an hour after yours."

"How'd you get your rat through?"

"Ferret," he said. "Bart took him. He owed me."

"Bart. Now there's a charmer. I can only imagine what he told you."

"That you asked him to drive you to Chicago and promised a blow job for the effort. Said you got pissed when he told you he wouldn't do that to me."

Sally shook her head. "I should have kicked him in the balls instead of breaking his nose." She stood and slung her pack over a shoulder. "Hey, you're not wearing your coat," she said.

"Bart's got it."

"Well, he said he was a lucky guy." Sally stuck out her hand. "Jake, it was fun. Thanks for checking on me. But I'm okay. And I hope your Chicago friend will be, too."

Jake reluctantly took her hand. "You know, you could change your flight."

Sally shook her head. "I don't think so."

"Wait," Jake said and found a pen in his pack. He pulled a piece of paper from his wallet and scribbled on it. "Here's my cell and the place I'm staying. Just in case you need to crash."

"Jake," she said. "You've already got one terminal friend. You don't need another."

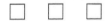

The street was busy. That part she remembered. But Sally didn't recognize the door to the townhouse. She remembered it being a different color and had forgotten it had a knocker. She rechecked the number before she rang the bell. They had lived there less than a year when Sally had left. The tree her father had planted next to the granite steps was now a good fifteen feet tall. She remembered watching him muscle the root ball into the hole.

She rang the bell again and shifted the pack on her shoulder. She wore a shirt with long sleeves and buttoned cuffs. She saw a curtain move, then heard the lock release. Her heart was thumping. A middle-aged woman opened the door. "Yes?"

"I'm looking for Mrs. Harrison," Sally said. "Does she still live here?"

"The Captain's wife?" the woman asked.

"Yes."

The woman's eyes searched Sally's. "Do you know her?"

"I'm her daughter."

The woman took an almost imperceptible step back. "I see," she said. "Sally is it?"

"Yes. Sally."

The woman nodded. "Perhaps you should come in."

Inside, the only thing familiar to Sally was the carved newel post at the bottom of the stairs. It was a smaller space than she remembered. The woman motioned to a settee. It was a somber red, upholstered in a heavy brocade. Crocheted doilies protected the arms. A mantel clock ticked the seconds. Sally didn't remember the mantel. Nor the fireplace. It was as if she'd never been in the room.

"You're the one who disappeared," the woman said.

"Yes, I suppose I am."

"That was cruel."

Sally swallowed. "There were reasons."

The clock ticked more seconds—slow seconds.

"I wouldn't know. I only saw what happened after you left."

Tick. Tick.

"Does my mother still live here?"

Tick.

"No, she doesn't."

"Do you know where she is?"

"Does it make any difference?" the woman said.

"Who are you?" Sally asked.

"You left a long time ago. It was like you'd been kidnapped. But no contact, no ransom demands, no proof of life."

"Where's my father?"

"I haven't seen him since the trial."

"What trial?"

The woman straightened the doily on the arm of her chair. She smoothed it out, patting it. "Your leaving caused a lot of pain," she said.

"What happened?"

"I was a friend of your mother's," the woman said. "I discovered her. When she didn't answer the door the second day, I used the key she'd given me. I found her and called the police."

Sally was short of breath. Her vision blurred and she felt dizzy. Closing her eyes made it worse. The throbbing started again deep in the back of her head. She gripped the arm of the chair and forced herself to breathe. "Is she dead?"

The woman abruptly stood. "I think you should leave now," she said.

"Tell me what happened," Sally said.

"You need to leave now." The woman picked up a phone. "You have no business here. You need to leave my house."

Sally tried to stand. A wave of vertigo swept over her. She fell back onto the settee.

"I'm calling the police now," the woman said. She punched in 9-1-1. "I have an intruder!" she cried into the mouthpiece. "She's forced her way in!" She disconnected, put the phone down, then walked to the door. "You only have a few minutes," she said.

Sally stood, still dizzy, but able to navigate. "Why won't you tell me?"

"Because you don't deserve to know," the woman said. "Why should you know when they didn't?" The woman held the door open. "I'd run if I were you."

As Sally stepped into the sun, the woman pushed the door shut behind her. Sally heard the lock fall into place. She held the railing as she made her way down the steps.

It was a gorgeous afternoon. Sunny. Warm. Perfect. A couple of doors down, two young moms sat on the steps talking, their preschool daughters playing on the sidewalk below them. A teen on a bike rode past. Aside from her father's tree, Sally didn't remember the shrubbery along the foundation of the house or the one next to it. It was all foreign. Nothing she had ever seen.

She steadied herself before she let go of the railing and crossed to the curb. She remembered it was a noisy street, but this afternoon, despite the traffic, the sounds were muffled as if she were underwater. She felt hot, flushed. She flagged a cab.

"Where to?" the driver asked as he pulled into the traffic.

"I don't know," she said.

"Gotta go somewhere."

"Just drive," she said as a Chicago patrol car raced past them.

Sally lit another cigarette. It was her third in a row. From her perch on the step, she watched the traffic slow with the end of rush hour. It was dusk, the day after her encounter at the house. The previous night she'd splurged on a downtown hotel and spent several hours in the confessional of the lobby pub. The woman bartender was Sally's age and practiced in feigning the sincere interest that preceded absolution. It was noon before Sally checked out to wander the streets of the Loop.

Sally lit a fourth cigarette from the ash of the third. The streetlights started to flicker on. She almost didn't recognize Jake when he rounded the corner two houses away. He wore a jean jacket and a baseball cap. He stopped at the bottom of the stairs.

"Hi," he said.

"New look," she said. "Cubs hat, nice touch."

"My friend's a big fan. Gave it to me. I promised to wear it proudly."

Sally leaned on her pack. "I was thinking," she said, flicking the ash off her cigarette. "If the invite's still good, maybe I could crash with you for a day or two. Figure since you lost your rat, you might appreciate a little company."

"Ferret."

"Yeah, that's what I meant."

Jake sat next to her on the step. "Been here long?"

She shook her head. "Half hour or so." She leaned forward, arms on knees.

"Hey," he said. "You've added to the gallery." A bandage covered an area near her wrist.

"Yeah," she said as she started to remove the gauze. "It's been a couple of hours. I'm supposed to put ointment on it."

"Looks like a woman," he said. "Thought you were going to use that last space for that asshole boyfriend."

"Changed my mind. Besides, I still have room on the other arm."

"Hey," said Jake. "She's looking at you."

"Yeah," Sally said. "She is."

THE NEIGHBORS

Newt Snyder took his time aiming. He was in his driveway leaning against the side rail of his Ford pickup. The streetlamp had been out for weeks. He was in the shadows, just like they'd trained him for Iraq. He took a low breath, let it half out, and squeezed the trigger. There was hardly a sound. The drone of his neighbor's air pump covered the pop of the silencer. Right between the eyes. The head snapped, then wobbled. A second shot and it started to deflate. In less than a minute the whole thing would be over.

Newt lowered the rifle and retreated into his house. It was a small place, cheaply built in the early fifties—a cottage with city water and sewer, gas, two bedrooms, a leaky roof, and a car port. Like all the others on the block. He tossed his coat on the couch and watched from behind the curtains as the inflatable Santa-on-a-motorcycle pancaked onto the snow. Three other airless Christmas figures lay in puddles of light around it, each aglow from a bulb under the plastic. One had been a snowman, another a tree. The largest had been a four-foot snow globe with a carousel inside—three little unicorns carrying an elf, an Elmo, and some other critter Newt didn't recognize. They had revolved inside the transparent shell while Christmas music played from a speaker sitting on the side step of a big, red Peterbilt cab backed into the driveway. His neighbor's front door burst open.

"Aw, shit!" the man yelled and spiked a beer can into the snow. "Goddamn fuckin' kids."

Newt's neighbor, Frank Brevic, wasn't a tall man, but he was built like a bear—barrel chest, short legs, big arms. He walked like a bear, too. Except for the mullet, if you covered him with fur he'd fool a naturalist. The man seldom wore a coat. He favored vests that showed the tattoos on his biceps and forearms. If the temperature dipped close to freezing, he'd wear a sweatshirt underneath, but that was it.

"It's all in the head," he'd once said to Newt. "You just concentrate on not shivering. That's where you lose your body heat." Brevic had been army. Two rotations in Iraq just like Newt. No shivering there.

Newt opened his door and yelled across the yard. "Hey, Brevic! What's the problem?"

"Fuckin' bastards." He stood in the snow, hands clenched in fists. "No fuckin' spirit of fuckin' Christmas."

Newt put his coat back on and went outside. Brevic was examining the Santa head. "Look at this," he said sticking his finger into the hole between Santa's eyes. "Fuckin' head shot."

"Clean."

"You got a gun, Newt?"

"Yeah. Why?"

"Cause if you see the bastards before I do, I want you to shoot their fuckin' balls off." He threw the plastic to the ground, then yanked the power cord off his porch. The music stopped and the pools of light disappeared, but the front of Brevic's house was still illuminated with rows of white bulbs that traced its outline.

They were strung along the soffits and around the frames of the windows. The chimney was highlighted with a Santa display, the old-fashioned kind, a rigid plastic 3-D figure lit from the inside and fastened to the brick with a clothesline.

Brevic kicked the snow. Newt noticed he was barefoot.

"Feet cold?" Newt asked.

Brevic looked down at his toes in the snow. "Can't tell anymore," he said. "Since Iraq, I don't have any feeling in 'em."

Newt grimaced. "Want a beer?"

Brevic shrugged but followed Newt into the house, leaving wet footprints all the way into the kitchen. Newt took two bottles out of the refrigerator. They twisted off the caps and clinked the necks.

"Merry Christmas," Newt said.

"Yeah, what's left of it."

They each took a healthy swallow.

"Shame about your yard display," said Newt. "You gonna replace them?"

Brevic shook his head. "I've patched them twice already. That's enough. Maybe I'll just get more lights for the house."

Newt nodded.

"So how come no feeling in the feet?" Newt asked.

Brevic shrugged again. "Nerve damage. Last tour. Shrapnel in my back. Pretty numb from the knees down."

"I'm surprised you can walk," said Newt.

Brevic smiled. "So are the sons-a-bitch docs." He took a sip. "I'm not supposed to be barefoot. Too easy to hurt 'em without realizing it."

Brevic looked out the window. "Hey, you can see right into my kitchen," he said. "That could be embarrassing."

Newt looked away. "Don't worry. I got better things to do."

Brevic looked around the room. "Opposite layout to mine."

"I think they just had one basic floor plan and flipped every other house," said Newt.

"Same gas stove." They sat at the table. "Yours work?"

Newt nodded.

"Mine's got a leak," said Brevic. "Landlady's too cheap to replace it so I just shut off the damn valve. Been using propane and an army camp stove."

"Better than MREs," said Newt.

"Sometimes," Brevic said and looked down the hall. "Two bedroom, right?"

"And one tiny bath."

"Ever think about getting outta this fuckin' neighborhood?" Brevic asked.

"All the time," said Newt.

Brevic leaned forward, elbows on knees. "Me too. All the fuckin' time. I think that's why I stay on the road so much. Fantasize sometime about just going AWOL and not coming back."

Frank Brevic was an independent. He owned his own rig but contracted with the majors, spending three weeks a month hauling auctioned cars all over the map.

"Ever have one fall off the back?" Newt asked him once.

"No, but I seen it happen," Brevic had said, then laughed as he told about some twenty-year-old forgetting to chain a high-end SUV. "First bump out of the yard and that fucker slid right off. Slow motion like. Last I heard the kid drives fruit and shit."

"Brevic, you in here?" a woman yelled from the front door.

"Yeah?"

"You driving me to work or what?"

Brevic grimaced and looked at Newt. "Yeah, I'm driving you." He downed the rest of the bottle and got up. "Wife's car is in the shop. Gotta go do my husbandly duty. Thanks for the beer."

"No problem," said Newt as Brevic barefooted it back into the snow.

A minute later, the Peterbilt fired up and Frank Brevic pulled out of his driveway with his wife Chelsea in the passenger seat. Newt watched from his front door.

Chelsea Brevic was a looker. Taller than Brevic and ten years younger. She bleached her hair and favored bright lipstick that left pink rings on the filters of her cigarettes. She wasn't overweight but had a fullness to her that stretched her clothes. Especially the tops. Chelsea was a waitress at a truck stop just off the interstate. It was a super stop, everything from Chelsea's restaurant to showers to truck detailing. Even mini-rooms where drivers could catch a couple of hours sleep or cheat some time with a working girl. Lots of traffic. An oasis in the desert of boredom for those riding the big rigs. It's where Frank Brevic met Chelsea Khalil almost six months earlier. And where Newt Snyder had met her a month before that—her first night on the job. Newt had taken a fancy to her. She reminded him of a woman he had flirted with during his tour in the Green Zone.

"Chelsea's not my real name," she had confessed to him the first time they had sex. She had a Middle Eastern accent that bordered on the exotic. "My real name is Iraq."

"That's your first name?"

"My father was a proud son of Iraq," she said as way of explanation. "He honored his homeland and cursed me with a stupid name. So I changed it when I came to the United States. I like how it sounded so American. Not like refugee."

Newt was an overnight mechanic at the truck stop. It was a trade he had adopted in high school and which served him well after the army pulled him off patrols. He became a diesel specialist, something that translated into job security when he came back to life as a civilian. A couple of times a week he'd take a 3:00 a.m. lunch at the restaurant. The night he met Chelsea, he was the only one at her counter. She made a point of leaning over so he could see down her blouse. It was an obvious move, but Newt liked the obvious. She told him she was going on break and invited him outside for a cigarette. They ended up in the sleeper of a five-year-old Kenworth that Newt had been servicing.

"Do you know why I decided to fuck you?" Chelsea asked after their frenzied first coupling.

"Why?" he said and stubbed out his cigarette in an ashtray on the floor.

"Your hands." She laced her fingers through his. "Your strong hands."

"You like my hands?"

"Hands of a man. Someone who could take care of a woman. I wanted to know what they would feel like on my body."

"They feel okay?"

She answered by kissing him and pushing him back onto the mattress.

"We need to get out of here," he said and sat up to pull on his jeans. "I told Bill I'd have this piece of shit out of here by now. He'd burn my ass if he found us ballin' in a customer's truck."

She had Newt on his back three nights in a row before she asked him for money.

"A hundred dollars," she said. "Just for tonight. The first two nights I fuck you for love."

"You crazy?" he asked. "I'm not giving you any fuckin' hundred dollars."

He was surprised that she looked hurt.

"Do you love me?" she asked.

"No, I don't love you," he said.

"Do you want to be my boyfriend? Take care of me?"

"Hell no."

"Then you should pay me. That's how things work. I give you sex, you pay me."

"Jeez," he said and looked out of the window. Bill was at the end of the bay hunting for something on the bench.

"Look, Chelsea," Newt said. "We had a good time. I didn't know you were on the clock. I'm sorry for any misunderstanding, but I ain't fuckin' paying you."

"Seventy-five," she said. "Or I'm telling Bill."

"No."

"Bill!" she yelled.

"Wait." Newt clamped his hand over her mouth. He looked out the window. Bill had turned toward the truck. Chelsea started to say something beneath Newt's hand. He shook her. "Quiet!" he rasped.

Bill turned back to the bench, picked a wrench, and then left.

Newt took his hand away.

"I think you should pay me the seventy-five dollars now," Chelsea said as she buttoned her blouse.

Newt stared at her. He took out his wallet and rifled through the bills. "I got thirty-six," he said. He threw two tens, three fives and a single on the mattress. She took the money, stuffed it in her cleavage, then climbed out of the cab without another word.

"Fuckin' bitch," he said.

Newt stayed away from the restaurant for a good week until one slow night when Bill dragged him across the lot for breakfast. Newt steered them to a booth away from Chelsea's counter. After they ate, Bill gave him the rest of the night off and headed back to the garage. Newt stayed, drank coffee, and watched Chelsea flirt with a driver at the counter. He saw her leave with him and return alone twenty minutes later. An hour after that, she left with another. When she returned the second time, she made eye contact with Newt just long enough to mouth a curse and give him the finger. That was almost seven months ago. Just before Frank Brevic took her bait.

Brevic had rented the house next door about the time Newt Snyder had been hustled by Iraq Chelsea Khalil. Newt admired Brevic's Peterbilt. The man had customized it nicely and kept it clean. Lots of drivers didn't keep their rigs clean. Brevic was not long back in the states. Kept to himself. It was two weeks before he mumbled a hello when Newt waved one morning coming home from work.

Newt was in the restaurant the night Brevic met Chelsea. He watched Brevic pay his counter bill and duck out the side door with her. But this time, she didn't come back. Newt stopped in an hour later to fill his thermos. Still no sign of her. "It was slow," said the other waitress. "She left early."

Later that morning after Newt was home, he caught a glimpse of Chelsea in Brevic's kitchen. She was laughing. A week after that, Chelsea Khalil had moved in. She and Brevic were married before the end of the month.

Now, half a year later, Newt never caught anyone laughing in the Brevic household. Brevic was sullen and Newt knew that Chelsea still moonlighted among the rigs outside the restaurant.

"You're a sorry bastard," Newt said as he watched Brevic's tail lights disappear down the block.

Newt pulled on a black sweatshirt and went outside. He stood for a moment in the shadows by his truck. With the dead streetlight, it was pretty dark, even with the holiday bulbs that hung from Brevic's house. Newt went to the end of his driveway, then followed the sidewalk onto Brevic's porch. The door was locked, but the cheap hardware was easy to defeat with a putty knife that Newt slid into the crack between the door and frame. The door opened and Newt slipped inside.

It wasn't the first time Newt had reconned Brevic's house. He'd slipped in once before when Brevic was on the road and Chelsea was working the restaurant. That time she almost caught him when she came home with one of her customers. He barely made it out the back window. He had rewarded himself by hanging in the yard and watching through the gauze of Brevic's bedroom curtain as Chelsea earned her money. Afterward, he felt exhilarated. "Like being shot at," he wrote in his journal.

Newt headed for the bedroom. It was a mess. Unmade bed and dirty clothes on the floor. He looked in a nightstand drawer. Same pills he'd found before. Two bottles with antidepressants, an expired antibiotic, and a wheel of birth control. She was almost out. The prescriptions were written for "Iraq." He hadn't noticed that before. He reached farther into the drawer and found a vibrator. "This is new," he said and turned it on. The batteries were low. "Well, Brevic, looks like you ain't getting the job done." He shut it off and tossed it back. In the other nightstand, he found a pack of condoms and a pack of cigarettes.

Newt checked the bathroom. The sink was small like his. Two worn toothbrushes were on the rim fighting for space with a deformed tube of toothpaste. In the cabinet above, two sets of shaving supplies, an open package of tampons, and half a dozen bottles of pills—two for Brevic, the rest for Iraq. Pain killers and other medications he didn't recognize. A hair dryer was on the back of the toilet along with a bottle of contact lens cleaner and a box of tissues. In the linen closet Newt found Brevic's gun in a stack of towels. It was loaded. Newt checked the safety and shoved it back into the terrycloth.

He returned to the bedroom and went through the dresser drawers where he had been interrupted the last time. Hers were on the bottom—sexy lingerie and skimpy panties. He held up one pair, a leopard print with a thong back. He pocketed them and felt through the rest, finding another vibrator nestled among the underwear. In the next drawer he found two envelopes. One was stuffed with cash. He counted it out—over 8,000 dollars in mixed bills. He wondered if his thirty-six were among them.

The other envelope was a collection of Polaroids. They featured a naked Chelsea in a number of poses with and without anonymous partners. Newt sat on the edge of the bed and thumbed through them. The photos were crude and amateur but their effect was electric, and Newt enjoyed feeling their energy. Until he got to one surprising shot of Chelsea playing alone on a couch. It was the couch in his living room.

Newt jumped when he heard the rumble of Brevic's truck pulling into the driveway. He stuffed everything back into their envelopes and shoved them into the drawer. He unlocked the window, but it wouldn't open. It was stuck, frozen by the ice that coated the outside sill. He heard the truck rev, then go silent. Newt tried to loosen the window by pounding the frame with the heel of his hand, but it only cracked the pane. He heard Brevic unlocking the door. Newt turned his face away from the window and elbowed the glass. It shattered.

"What the fuck?" Brevic said from the kitchen. Newt heard him coming down the hall and slammed the bedroom door. He jammed a chair under the knob and dove out the window.

"Shit!" he said as he hit the ground harder than expected. He got up and staggered across the snow in the direction opposite his house. He made it across three backyards before he realized he was limping. He turned into the street. No sign of Brevic. Newt kept to the shadows and circled the block, approaching his house from the side away from his neighbor's. He let himself into the back and stood in his kitchen, hands on knees, catching his breath. "Shit!" he repeated between gasps. "Too close."

The overhead light flickered on. "Closer than you fuckin' think," Brevic said behind him.

Newt felt the pressure of a gun on the side of his neck.

"Move slowly," Brevic said. "While you're down there, take off your boots."

As Newt untied his boots, he saw blood. One of his pant legs was slit. He had cut himself jumping out the window. The adrenaline had damped the pain during his flight, but now, in his kitchen, he felt it starting to burn.

"Turn 'em upside down," said Brevic. "Let's see the pattern on them soles."

Newt did as he was told.

"You fuckin' asshole," Brevic said as he kicked Newt to the floor.

"Jeez, man!" Newt yelled as he tried to shield himself.

"What the fuck you doing in my house?" Brevic was barefoot but let go another kick that connected with Newt's injured leg. Newt rolled in pain. Brevic kicked at him again. "Fuckin' going through my drawers!"

"What the fuck you talking about?" Newt said, trying to protect his bloody leg.

"What the fuck I'm talking about?" asked Brevic. "What the fuck I'm talking about?" He reached down and yanked Chelsea's panties out of Newt's pocket. "Fuckin' pervert." He got ready for another kick.

"Don't!" yelled Newt, curling up to protect himself. "Stop!"

Brevic hesitated. "Aw, fuck," he said. "I broke my fuckin' toe again." He sat on the floor with a thud. Newt looked over. Brevic's big toe was bent sideways. "Shit."

Newt sat up against the refrigerator. His leg was throbbing. His hands were bloody. He could see the gash in his leg. It was big enough for stitches. He grabbed a dishtowel hanging from a drawer and pressed it over the wound.

"Doc's going to fuckin' kill me," said Brevic. "She told me not to go barefoot." He laid his gun on the floor and reached for his toe. He jerked it back into place with a snap. Newt grimaced. Brevic picked up his gun. "I should just fuckin' kill you and be done with it."

"Don't," Newt said, raising a palm toward his neighbor. "Please."

Brevic held the pistol at arm's length, aiming right between Newt's eyes.

"A nice, clean head shot," said Brevic.

Newt raised both hands in surrender. "Look, man," he said. "I'm sorry. It was a dumbass thing to do."

Brevic held the gun steady for a few long seconds, then bent his elbow and fired into the ceiling. Newt flinched. Plaster snowed over them and a chunk the size of a dinner plate fell onto the floor at Brevic's feet. He kicked at it with his heel. "Fuck."

Newt reached back to his leg. The bleeding had stopped. The two men sat there for a moment. Brevic smiled.

"What was you planning on doing with them panties? Wear 'em?"

"I don't know," said Newt. "I wasn't really thinking."

"She told me about it, you know."

"What."

"How you fuckin' stiffed her."

"I didn't stiff her. We just had a little misunderstanding."

"Yeah," said Brevic. "Thirty-six dollars." He reached toward Newt's leg and lifted the towel. "Shit, man. You need to clean that thing and get it sewed up. You got some isopropyl?"

"In the bathroom."

Brevic got up. He came back with the bottle and a roll of gauze. He grabbed a knife off the counter and knelt down. He slit the rest of Newt's pant leg and exposed the wound.

"This might hurt a bit," Brevic said as he unscrewed the bottle top.

Newt gasped as Brevic poured the alcohol over the gash. He balled his fists and concentrated on staying conscious as the pain seared up his leg and into his gut. He was sweating. Brevic wrapped the bandage around the wound and tied it off.

"That'll hold you till we get there."

"Get where?" asked Newt, his hands shaking.

"The fuckin' VA, man."

"I don't need the VA."

"Suit yourself," said Brevic. "I'll sew it up here for you."

Newt looked at him.

"I can, you know. One of the many survival skills I brought back with me."

Newt shook his head.

"Then get your boots on."

Newt struggled, and Brevic helped him tie the laces.

"Come on," Brevic said, pulling him to his feet.

Newt's leg was on fire, but he made it to Brevic's driveway and into the Peterbilt. Brevic fished a pair of socks and boots from behind the driver's seat and put them on. "If I walk in there barefoot, they won't let me out," he said.

Brevic started the engine. They rolled onto the street. Neither said a word for a block and a half.

"I ain't much good below the waist," said Brevic. "Fuckin' shrapnel numbed everything."

Newt sank into his seat.

"Chelsea's been real good about it. She don't really expect anything from me in that department." Brevic maneuvered the Peterbilt onto the boulevard that led downtown. "We play around with her toys and shit, but when it comes down to the nitty-gritty, she just needs a little outside entertainment. Letting her keep working, well, seems the least I can do. Fact she gets paid for it's a fuckin' bonus."

Newt lowered the window to let the cold air dry the sweat on his face. "Why you telling me this shit?"

"To let you know that I know," said Brevic. "Let you know she ain't doin' stuff behind my fuckin' back."

Brevic stopped for a light. They sat in silence until it changed. "It don't bother you?" asked Newt.

"Fuck, man. I didn't say that." Brevic started through the intersection.

"I saw the pictures," said Newt.

Brevic shrugged

"You take 'em?"

"She likes to pose. Keeps hoping to get one in *Hustler*. You know, 'photo by husband.'"

"You took one on my couch."

Brevic laughed. "That's the one she wanted to send in."

They parked in a lot across from the ER. Newt's leg was aflame. He could barely put pressure on it. Brevic helped him down from the cab. Newt leaned on Brevic more than he wanted. By the time they got inside, Newt was dripping in sweat. A nurse got him a wheelchair. Brevic got him some water.

The ER was crowded. Damaged vets in all states of disrepair. It took close to two hours before someone looked at him. The pain had settled into a steady throb, nothing he couldn't handle with concentration. He'd been hurt worse than this. The bleeding had stopped, but the wound was deeper than he thought. When the doctor started examining it, the fire returned. Newt gripped the sides of the table and lay back on his elbows, gritting his teeth. The doctor emptied a syringe with multiple stabs around the gash until the fire went out. There was embedded glass the doctor had to remove and then a dozen stitches. By the time they were finished, Newt's leg was wrapped tightly, an ace bandage holding it all together.

"Try to stay off it for a couple of days," the doctor said.

Brevic wheeled Newt back to the truck and helped him into the cab.

"Thanks," Newt mumbled after they'd settled into the seats.

"No problem," Brevic grunted and started the engine.

They got back to the boulevard before Brevic said, "But you could do me a favor."

Newt shrugged.

"Help me kill her."

It had snowed again. A good six inches. It had been four days since Brevic had asked Newt to help him frag his wife. Newt was pretty much back on his feet, but avoided going outside for fear of running into his neighbor, even after the guy cleared both their sidewalks and driveways with his snow blower, finishing off the front steps by hand.

It was 6:00 p.m. Newt had to go to work. Bill had threatened to can him if he took any more time off, leg or no leg. Newt eased on his boots. He looked out the window to check Brevic's driveway. The Peterbilt had been gone all day. Chelsea's car was back from the shop—a ten-year-old beater with a driver's door that didn't match. As long as she parked in the driveway, Newt knew Brevic was on the road. Newt was about to open the door when he saw Chelsea heading toward her car. He'd wait until she left.

She slid behind the wheel. The motor barely turned over. It groaned a couple of times, then stopped altogether. She got out and slammed the door. He was surprised when he saw her cross the driveway toward his porch. She rang the bell.

He stood still, hoping she'd give up quickly. But she knew he was home because his truck was outside. She rang again, then knocked. He took a breath and opened it.

"You going to work?" she asked.

He nodded.

"I need a ride."

She didn't say anything for half the trip. She sat next to him, seatbelt tight, arms crossed. At a stoplight he caught her looking at him. She smiled.

"I still like your hands," she said.

It was warm in the truck. Chelsea unzipped her coat. Beneath the winter padding, she showed cleavage.

"Don't you get cold?" Newt asked.

"I keep a sweater at work," she said. "Besides, being in and out of the kitchen keeps me hot."

He shrugged.

"How is your leg?" she asked. "He told me you hurt it."

"Leg's fine," he said.

"He told me you hurt it in our house."

"It's fine," he repeated.

"I am embarrassed," she said. "He told me you saw the pictures."

Newt looked at her. She looked away.

"He makes me take the pictures," she said. "It's not my idea." She looked at him again, no trace of a smile.

Newt stopped for a light. "Didn't look like you were objecting too much," he said.

"He beat me if I don't pose for him. Pictures don't show that." She crossed her arms again.

Newt pulled onto the highway. "So the hustling part's okay," he said. "Just not the pictures."

"I marry him," she said. "I thought I have someone to take care of me. Someone who understood. But he chooses men for me to bring home. Makes me do things."

"Like play on my couch?"

She looked out the side window. "I told him you and I were lovers once. So he broke into your house and had me sit there. He was going to give you the picture to show you're no longer the big man."

Newt shook his head. "Chelsea," he said. "You're so full of shit I'm surprised yon don't choke." Before he could say anything else, she punched him in the face.

"Jesus!" he yelled as he swerved onto the shoulder and back. "Fuck, woman! You trying to kill us?" He touched his jaw where she connected. "Fuck." He raised his arm when he saw her move again but nothing happened. He looked over. She was crying, sobbing into her hands. "Oh, jeez," he said. "I'm the one should be crying."

"You don't understand either," she said between sobs. "You just think I'm a whore."

"Well ain't you?" He thought she was going to hit him again, but she took a tissue from her pocket instead and blew her nose.

"You don't know how hard it has been," she said. "I come here alone. No family. No friend. No dollars. I do what I need to stay alive. I look for someone to take care of me so I can be normal. But I made a bad choice." She blew her nose again.

Newt looked at her. She pulled another tissue from her pocket and dabbed at her eyes.

"Nicely done," he said. "You almost convinced me."

"You are a bastard," she said and started to cry again.

He slowed for the exit. By the time they reached the truck plaza, she was quiet, facing her window. He parked near the garage and shut off the engine. She didn't move.

"We're here," he said. She turned to him.

"I am sorry for what you think of me," she said.

"Well," Newt nodded. "Maybe you can't help it. I'm sorry for making you cry."

He opened his door, but she reached over and put her hand on his leg. "Wait."

Newt held the handle.

"I have to tell you something," she said.

He closed the door. "What?"

"He is only half a man. From the war. He can't be a true husband."

"Chelsea, that ain't none of my business." She moved her hand up his leg. He grabbed her wrist. "Look," he said. "I know what you're trying to sell here, but I'm not buying."

She smiled at him. "Did you like when we were lovers?"

"We were never lovers," Newt said and put her hand on the seat.

She moved her hand back to his leg. "Sex, then. When we had sex. Did you like our sex?"

Newt looked at her. The smile had faded. It was a real question. "Yeah," he said. "It was good."

"Thank you," she said and pulled her hand away.

"You're welcome." He started to open the door again.

"Wait," she said.

"What?"

She rested her finger tips on his thigh. "May I give you a kiss to thank you?"

Newt chuckled. "You gonna charge me for it?"

She leaned over and kissed him. It was a gentle brush at first. But she slid across the seat and kissed him again.

"Shit," Newt said. She kissed him a third time. He felt himself warming to her touch. He reached up and put his hand against her cheek. She sighed. He moved his hand to her breast. She whimpered, then took his hand in hers.

"This is not a good place," she said.

"You want me to see if we got a sleeper in the garage?" he asked.

"No," she said. "I don't want to do that."

"What then?"

"Maybe you give me a ride home after my shift?"

It was a slow night. For all his harping, Bill had little for Newt to do. By midnight, Bill told him he could leave. Newt's leg was throbbing, but he walked over to the diner. He sat at Chelsea's counter. She leaned on her elbows in front of him. It was hard not to look at her breasts.

"I can get off early," she said. "Have something to eat, then I'll meet you at your truck"

He ordered one of their specials. When he finished, he paid the bill and waited in his truck. He was listening to an '80s station when she opened the passenger door and climbed inside. Without a word she pushed herself against him and kissed him, pulling his hand against her. "Take me home," she said.

They rode again in silence. This time she was close to him, nuzzling his neck, her hand inside his thigh. When he pulled into his driveway, she led him into his house. "Did you like my pictures?" she asked as they balled on his couch. They did it again in his bed. Afterward, they shared a cigarette.

"Thank you," she said.

"For what?" he asked.

"For making love to me."

He didn't argue about her choice of words. She took a long drag and blew smoke over his chest.

"Can I ask you something?" she said, handing him the cigarette.

He flicked the ash into a bedside ashtray. "Sure."

"A favor," she said as she nestled her body against his.

"You can ask," he said as he handed her back the cigarette.

She took another drag. As she exhaled against his ear she whispered, "Will you help me kill him?"

Brevic was back. His truck was in the driveway, and Chelsea's car was parked at the curb. Newt felt a prisoner in his own house. At work the night before, Chelsea had stopped by the garage twice looking for him. Both times he saw her coming and hid behind a rig.

"You got something going on with that bimbo from the diner?" Bill asked after her second visit.

"We're neighbors," Newt told him. "Probably looking for a ride home."

"I'm not so sure," said Bill.

That morning when he drove home, Newt parked down the block from his house and snuck in the back door. The Peterbilt was in Brevic's driveway. Newt kept his lights off and watched the street from behind his curtains. Chelsea came home just before dawn. Newt moved to the kitchen. From the shadows he watched her rinse a coffee cup in the sink. When she turned off the tap, he saw Brevic slip behind her, put his arms around her, and kiss her neck.

She turned and embraced him. She left the cup on the counter as Brevic led her out of the room.

Newt managed to avoid them for another day. But returning from a beer run, he saw Brevic's Peterbilt in his mirror. His neighbor followed him all the way home and pulled into the driveway as Newt was climbing out of his truck.

"Hey, Newt." Brevic waved from his yard. "Haven't seen you for a while. Come on over. I owe you a beer."

"Can't right now," Newt said. "Maybe a little later."

Brevic came across the drive. He glanced over his shoulder. "I got it figured out." But before he could explain, his wife pulled up in front of the house. "Shit."

Chelsea took a grocery bag off the passenger seat and started up the driveway. When she saw Newt, she went back to the car and got something from the dash. Newt shifted his six pack from one hand to the other.

"We have some of your mail by mistake," she said. "I was going to stick it in your slot, but since you're here . . ." She handed it to him.

"Thanks," Newt said.

"Well, good to see you," said Brevic. "If I don't catch you later, thanks again for the beer." He turned and headed toward his house. Chelsea started to follow but hesitated.

"I have something to tell you," she said, then looked over her shoulder after Brevic. "He beat me again last night. I am afraid."

"Chelsea?" Brevic yelled from the porch. "You gonna fix dinner?"

"Yes," she called back. "I'm coming." When she turned back to Newt, he thought she was going to cry. "I know what I need to do," she said, then ran across the driveway and into her house.

Inside his kitchen, Newt took a beer from the six pack and twisted it open. He took a long drink and sat at the table. He looked at the mail Chelsea had handed him. One envelope was without a stamp. He opened it. It was the photo of her naked on his couch.

"Shit." Newt stuffed the picture back into the envelope and took another drink.

He had the night off, but shortly after dark he moved his truck down the block and snuck back into the house. He didn't want Brevic banging on the door after Chelsea left for work.

Chelsea did leave but was back a couple of hours later. She parked behind Brevic's truck. She wasn't alone. Someone slid out behind her, and arm-in-arm they went inside. Newt checked the view from his kitchen, but the lights were out.

He finished another beer and crawled into bed. He could still smell Chelsea on his sheets. It stoked his curiosity about what was happening a few dozen yards away. But he was tired, and before his fantasies could play out, he was asleep.

The explosion threw him across the room. He was under attack. He found himself pinned to the floor. Alarms whooped as he struggled to free himself. His bed was on top of him. He managed to push aside the mattress and box spring and elbowed himself across the floor before a second explosion blasted outside the perimeter. He covered the back of his head as debris rained over him, then he rolled to safety in the hall. His heart was pounding. It took a moment to get his bearings. There was glass on the floor. He looked through his bedroom door. The window had blown in bringing part of the frame with it. But instead of the cold of winter, there was heat, intense and searing. Brevic's house was on fire. Flames shot twenty feet in the air. Newt grabbed for his jeans and boots.

He made it onto the street, then stood and watched as Brevic's house deconstructed. By the time a fire crew arrived, the dwelling was a flaming skeleton. The crew kept the blaze from spreading to Newt's house, but it was clear that the water damage to his place would leave it uninhabitable. After the fire was out, the crew chief let him throw some things in a suitcase, then surrounded the site with yellow tape.

"What caused it?" Newt asked.

"Too early to tell for sure. Started in the kitchen. Gas leak, maybe."

"My neighbors," he said, not sure how to finish the sentence.

The chief pointed across the driveway. Two men were carrying a covered body on a stretcher. A second stretcher followed.

Newt felt his legs weaken. He sat on the curb.

"You okay?" asked the chief.

"Yeah," said Newt. "Yeah, I'm fine."

"It never gets easy," said the chief.

"You need someone to identify them?" asked Newt.

The chief shook his head. "Not enough left."

The tears that came surprised Newt. They burned his eyes as he squeezed them away. He got to his feet and walked down the block. He threw his bag into his truck and headed to the garage. He'd stay there for a night or two until he figured out what had to be done.

Three months had passed. Newt had repaired his house and replaced his damaged furniture. When the last piece was delivered, he tacked Chelsea's picture above the dresser.

Brevic's landlady had the remains of the rental bulldozed. She sold the lot to a local developer who had already started construction on a small cottage. Between the insurance and the sale, Newt figured the old lady wasn't too sad about the fire.

At the end of each day when the construction crew left, Newt walked the shell and fantasized about moving up. Maybe it wasn't so bad here. He liked the neighborhood. It was quiet and easy to get to work. Maybe it wasn't that crazy an idea.

The day he made an offer on the house, he received a plain, hand-lettered envelope in the mail. There was a Mexican postmark but no return address. He sat in his kitchen and opened it. Inside, folded in a sheet of plain paper, he found two ten dollar bills, three fives and a single.

He spread the bills evenly in front of him, then got a beer. He raised the bottle in a silent salute and took a long drink.

WHY JIMMY MENDOZA HATED THE LATE TAMALE JONES

Despite his appropriate grieving at the funeral, Jimmy Mendoza had to admit he was glad the son of a bitch was dead. He stood by the closed casket and reached out to touch it as if to say a final goodbye. But he was really thinking he'd like to pop it open, make sure Tamale Jones was in there.

Tamale Jones. Born Tommy Lee. Age fifty-two. Not-so-respected businessman and city council member. Survived by a wife, three kids, and one mean dog. Not to mention two girlfriends who both thought he was getting a divorce, and a partner convinced he was stealing from their business. Which he was. Jimmy had figured that out shortly after Tamale talked him into doing the books.

"But you still did them, didn't you?" Jimmy could hear Tamale's voice. And it was true. Jimmy bitched about it but still did them. "Damn right you still did them."

Tamale Jones. Dropped like a rock in the middle of an argument with Kelly Bradley, one of his lady friends. She'd caught him having a romantic dinner in a quiet Italian restaurant with some skinny young thing. Surprised him when she walked in with a guy twenty years his junior, who ushered her through the door with a hand on her butt. Shocked the hell out of Tamale when she spotted him and headed straight for his table. Made a scene that ended with him clutching his chest and collapsing into his pasta without getting in the last word.

The fact that Kelly Bradley was Jimmy's ex had little to do with his feelings about Tamale. Kelly and Jimmy were a mistake from the get-go. And he'd long since wished her well in all her meanderings. Including her liaisons with the now deceased.

No, the reason Jimmy Mendoza loathed Tamale Jones was more complicated than that.

"Oh, jeez. You're not gonna whine about the Angie Starr thing again are you?"

The voice was muffled but surprisingly clear. Jimmy looked around. No one was near him. Tamale's wife and kids stood off to the side talking with mourners, some of them well-wishers. She was dressed in appropriate black but let slip an occasional smile. She should smile, Jimmy thought. He knew about the policy she had on the bastard. Enough to continue living in the style to which she had accustomed herself.

"Open the damn lid," the voice said.

Jimmy grasped the edge of the casket. It lifted easier than he would have guessed. Tamale stared up at him. He looked like hell.

"What you expect?" he said. "I've been gone three days, for chrissake. They drain your blood, cake you with makeup. You wouldn't look so hot either."

"You're supposed to be dead," Jimmy said. "What kind of scam you pulling this time?"

"No scam," he said. "I am dead." He held up his hand. "Wanna feel?"

Jimmy shook his head.

"Yeah, I don't blame you." Tamale struggled into a sitting position. Swung his legs over the edge. Leaned back against the open lid.

"What the hell's going on?" Jimmy asked.

"You're thinking about telling our story without my side, that's all."

"It's not 'our' story," Jimmy said. "It's 'my' story. I'm the one got screwed."

Tamale grunted a laugh. "You didn't get close to getting screwed. That's one of the reasons you were always so pissed about it. Sit down," he said. "If you're gonna tell the damn story, you might as well be comfortable."

Jimmy looked around again. No one was paying attention. He sat next to Tamale.

"You see," Tamale said, "whenever you bitch to me about Angie Starr, you never get my part right. You never give me credit for what I did for you."

"Did for me? What'd you do for me?"

"Gave you an adventure you're still talking about, for one thing," he said. "Whose idea was it to drive to Texas anyway? I didn't hear you saying, 'Hey, I got a great idea, Tamale. Let's drive to Texas for the weekend. Come on, let's do something different.' Didn't hear any a those words coming outta your mouth."

"It's not about whose idea it was," Jimmy said. "It's about what happened when we got there."

"I'm just saying . . ." Tamale said, "I'm just saying if I hadn't talked your sorry ass into making the trip, you'd have nothing to look back on."

"You do this every time," Jimmy said. "You make it all about you. You make it your story. And it's *my* story."

"Hell it is," Tamale said. "I'm the one was facing life. Or worse. No statute of limitations in Texas for killing someone. I'm the one he fingered. If they'd found us, I was the one gonna be strapped to the gurney, not you. You'd be looking at a couple of years, tops. I'd be dead."

Jimmy looked at him. "Kind of moot, ain't it?"

Jimmy couldn't tell if Tamale smiled. His range of movement was limited. Hard to read anything on his face. The makeup was thick, waxy. It hid anything subtle. Jimmy waited for some smart-ass response, but there wasn't one. So he continued.

"All I'm saying . . ." Jimmy said, "All I'm saying is that you never acknowledged that *I* gave up something, too."

"I'm thirsty," said Tamale. "I need a drink."

"That's probably not a good idea."

"It's my funeral," said Tamale. "I can have a drink if I want one. I paid for a bar. Get us a couple a beers."

The adjacent room had a bar set up in the corner. Cash with a big tip jar. Most of the mourners had already been by. A number stood together swirling drinks in glasses. Jimmy nodded at Kelly, his ex, who was keeping her distance from Tamale's widow. Half of those in the place were badmouthing Tamale. Everyone had a story. Jimmy got two beers and headed back. Tamale stood by the flowers, reading the cards.

"Cheap bastards," he said when Jimmy handed him a bottle. "All I done for them, and they send this?" He pulled a bud from the stem. "I hated roses," he said. "Everyone knows I hated roses." He flicked it away from him.

"It's the thought," Jimmy said.

"Yeah, yeah," he said and raised his bottle. "To my death." He emptied the whole thing in one smooth movement.

"Jeez, Tamale. You didn't even swallow."

"Can't swallow," he said. "No swallowing muscles. I think they pulled everything out in the autopsy. Probably wrapped in my gut like gizzards in a turkey." He tossed the empty in the casket. "Let's get another."

They wandered to the bar. Tamale reached behind the bartender and pulled two beers from the ice. He twisted off the tops and poured one down his throat. He stuck the empty back in the ice, neck down.

"That helped," he said. "Let's mingle. I want to hear what these sonsabitches are saying about me."

There wasn't much good. After hearing the third version of how he'd screwed someone over, Tamale shook his head, then headed outside. Jimmy followed. They sat in the sun on the front steps.

"It's hot," Tamale said, loosening the top buttons on his shirt. The skin beneath was split and bloodless, a ragged incision was loosely held together with uneven stitches. "You got a cigarette?" he asked.

Jimmy handed him one and held the match while Tamale leaned forward to light it.

"Everyone got something out of me," Tamale said. "Everyone a them bastards got something. They forget that part." He looked at Jimmy. "Even you."

"It's not what I got, Tamale. It's what I shoulda got."

"You got a great story," he said.

"One I could never tell."

Tamale struggled to face Jimmy. "If you had," he said, "neither one of us woulda made it this far."

It had been an early February. Early February in the Midwest. Winds across the prairie. Snow. Ice. They'd been students at a university in the middle of Illinois. Big campus. Lots to do, but no place to get warm. Jimmy was a business major but fantasized about being a film student, a screenwriter. Had these illusions of seeing characters he created come to life on the big screen. Had even written a script, but too chickenshit to take a course or show anyone besides Tamale what he'd been doing.

The idea of driving to Texas for a long weekend was crazy. But when you're twenty, immortal, and searching for adventure, it's just the kind of idea that fuels action. They didn't tell anyone. They didn't want any hitchhikers, or worse, anyone talking them out of it. They left late on a Thursday afternoon, took turns driving straight through. It was just over a thousand miles from campus to Austin. Triple-A said sixteen hours, but they made it in less than fourteen.

They found a cheap motel near the interstate, slept all afternoon, then made plans for the Friday evening scene. They had their bogus IDs, a couple of hundred in cash, and a tourist map of the downtown area.

Sixth Street Austin was where they heard it happened. Music, art, women. They made the rounds of bars, drinking Texas beer and talking up the locals. Except many of the locals weren't so local. Some were students at the mama university a mile or so north, others were visitors in the capital for one or another reason.

That's when they met Angie Starr. She was a thirty-something D-list actress Jimmy had recognized from a TV movie and a tabloid article about a jealous boyfriend beating her on camera. She was with a bunch of people letting off steam after a long day on some low-budget film shoot.

"Here's your chance," Tamale had said. "Pitch her your script. See if she'll tumble."

She took a liking to Tamale, and before long invited them to a party in the hills west of town. Jimmy drove. Tamale and Angie lay on the back seat, groping each other.

It was a private home. Huge. Big pool. Separated from neighbors by lots of trees and shrubs. Some big music producer lived there, Angie had said. "Stevie Bell." A name that sounded vaguely familiar to them. He was the one financing the film. Austin had always been known for its music and film scene, something that conjured up independent musicians and filmmakers struggling against the big guys. And this seemed to be one of those big guys. Angie explained that someone had to make the money.

She gave them a tour of the place, leading Tamale by the hand through the guy's recording studio, then his office, which included a shooting range, and finally into a multi-car garage set up like an auto showroom. It held a collection of 1950s classics.

"This is my favorite," Angie said as she slipped behind the wheel of a white MG. Tamale sat next to her. "This is the one he promised me if the film we're doing makes any money."

She wrapped her fingers around the steering wheel and slid her hands over the wood as if making turns on a country road. Tamale's hand slid up her thigh. She turned and kissed him.

"Just what the fuck's going on down here?" some voice said from near the entrance.

Angie was startled. "Oh, Stevie," she said, pushing Tamale's hand off her leg. "Just showing the boys your toys."

A man carrying a half-empty bottle of vodka stumbled toward them. If this was the guy who owned the place, he was younger than Jimmy expected. Late twenties at the most. Lean. Long hair. Beard. T-shirt. Jeans. And boots with heels that added a good two inches to his height. Even with those, however, he was still a half-foot shorter than Jimmy.

"And just who are these boys?" he asked, waving the bottle toward them.

"They're from the university," she said. They hadn't told her which one. As she and Tamale got out of the car, she pointed at Jimmy. "He's a screenwriter."

"Everybody's a screenwriter," Stevie Bell said and took a swig from the bottle. He squinted at Jimmy. "Don't like anyone down here. Angie knows that."

"I'm sorry, Stevie," she said.

"I'll deal with you later."

"I just wanted to show them the car."

"Yeah, I bet you did." He grabbed a cloth from the workbench. "See, boys, Angie likes to sneak guys down here. Usually it's only one at a time, though."

"Stevie, it wasn't like that," she said, hugging herself. "Really."

Stevie Bell wiped off each door where Tamale and Angie had touched them. He stood back looking for other smudges.

"So, Mr. Screenwriter," he said. "Why don't you tell me a story? Always looking for a good story. "

"As a matter of fact," said Tamale, "he's got a finished script."

"That so." Stevie Bell picked up his vodka.

Tamale elbowed Jimmy.

"Yeah," Jimmy said, then recited the ninety-second synopsis he had practiced.

Stevie Bell took another swig. "It's stupid," he said, wiping his mouth with the back of his hand. "Lousy premise and an unsympathetic protagonist."

Jimmy flushed. It wasn't what he was hoping for.

"I don't know," said Angie. "I think it's kind a cute."

Without warning, Stevie Bell threw the bottle at her. It caught her on the side of the face. "Cute?" he yelled. "Cute ain't worth shit. And if I'd wanted your opinion, I'd a asked for it."

"Hey," said Tamale, taking a step toward him. "There's no need for that."

Stevie Bell turned and smiled. "You telling me how to act in my own house?"

"Where we are doesn't matter," said Tamale. "All I'm saying is you should take it easy."

Stevie Bell slid open a workbench drawer. "Where we are does matter," he said, pulling out a handgun. "You come into *my* house, paw *my* property, then tell me how I should act?" He raised the gun. "I think you boys look like intruders."

"Whoa," Tamale said, raising his palms. "We don't want any trouble."

"Too late for that."

"Stevie, honey," said Angie. "Please put that away."

"Shut up!" He surprised her with a backhand that dropped her to her knees.

What happened next Jimmy only recalled as a blur. There was some sort of scuffle. At one point, Jimmy had the gun. Then lost it. Then Tamale had the gun. Then lost it. Jimmy remembered being on the floor. He remembered hearing a shot. Then another. And the next thing Jimmy knew, he was alone in the driveway. It may have been as long as a minute before Tamale stumbled out behind him.

"She's dead," he said. "We need to get out of here." Tamale kept an eye on the mirror as they headed back to town. When he was satisfied no one was following, he slowed to near the speed limit.

"What just happened?" Jimmy asked.

It was a long couple of seconds before Tamale answered. "We don't know what happened," he said. "We weren't here. As a matter of fact, we were never in Texas. We were in Illinois. We just heard about this guy on the news."

It took a minute for Jimmy to digest what Tamale was trying to tell him. They drove to the motel, threw their stuff in the car, and got on the highway. They took turns driving and were back in Illinois by midafternoon the next day.

Tamale wouldn't talk about what happened in the garage, but that Sunday afternoon, he handed Jimmy a page from the *Chicago Tribune*. It was a short article about an Austin music and film producer named Stevie Bell being arrested in the shooting death of his actress girlfriend, Angie Starr. He claimed innocence, his lawyer saying another man, one of a pair of college students attending a party at the house, was responsible. But references to Stevie Bell's violent nature and a previous arrest for domestic abuse seemed to seal his fate.

It took almost a year before Stevie Bell went to trial, and in those months, Tamale and Jimmy told no one about the trip to Austin. The trial itself was popular in the entertainment press. Over the six weeks of motions and testimony, there were mentions of two college guys in a bar that Angie had met earlier that evening. But there were always college guys in bars. They were never identified, and no credible evidence was presented that they even existed.

There was a smudged handprint on the pistol, but Stevie Bell liked to show off his guns, and there were fragments of other prints, including one identified as Angie's. It led to one desperate defense move that she had actually fired the weapon herself. The prosecutor used it as a wedge to open a whole line of testimony about Stevie Bell's penchant for mixing guns and sex. One witness testified how Stevie Bell would always come to bed armed. Another about how he'd held a gun in her mouth during one possessed coupling.

And finally there was *The Self-Portrait*. The photograph was never published, but euphemistic descriptions had Angie servicing Stevie Bell while he stood smugly with a pistol to her temple. Some of the testimony was suppressed. Some was disregarded. But in total it drew a picture of an egocentric crazy who easily could have killed Angie Starr in a moment of passion, or anger, or pleasure, and then tried to fabricate a story to fit the circumstances.

After three days of deliberation, the jury found him guilty of voluntary manslaughter. He was sentenced to fifteen years.

"That shoulda been the end of it," Tamale said to Jimmy as they sat on the steps of the funeral home. He sucked hard on his cigarette, the smoke seeping from between the careless stitches in his chest. "He shoulda just bided his time and been grateful they didn't fry him."

But it wasn't the end of it. While he was doing time, Stevie Bell wrote a novel, a best seller. It wasn't about the shooting. It was something "stupid" and had "a lousy premise and an unsympathetic protagonist." It was the story Jimmy had told to him in the minutes before Angie was shot. He even used Jimmy's character names. And before he got out of prison—several years early for good behavior—he had turned the novel into a film script. On his release, he directed the movie. It was widely talked about and financially successful. And in all the promotion he did for it, Stevie

Bell openly credited the two college boys who had murdered his girlfriend. It was a taunt.

But it didn't work. Tamale kept Jimmy quiet.

"The sequel was a nice touch," Tamale said.

The sequel. Another moneymaker. Jimmy's original characters with a new plot that included a reenactment of Angie's death, the protagonist struggling with two young intruders who fire the shot that kills his fiancée. The scene was stunning in its portrayal of Tamale and Jimmy. The physical resemblance was accurate enough to spark one of their old college housemates to e-mail a link to the movie scene with a smart-ass joke questioning their whereabouts that weekend.

"You done reminiscing?" Tamale asked.

"I'm not reminiscing," Jimmy said. "I'm just wondering what could a been if you hadn't screwed up my big chance."

"What big chance? The only reason that piece a shit got produced was because the asshole got a lot of press. If you really wanted to be a screenwriter, why didn't you write something else? I'll tell you why," he said, not waiting for a response. "Because you were a lousy writer. Your stuff was crap. You never had any 'big chance.' I didn't take anything away from you. I *gave* you something. I got you outta there. I kept you safe."

Tamale stubbed the cigarette out on the step next to him. "I gotta get back inside. I'm starting to melt. And they're gonna take the casket to the cemetery."

Jimmy stood. Tamale put out a hand for help getting up, but Jimmy ignored it.

Back in the viewing room, one of the funeral directors was telling those planning to follow the hearse how to stay close to the car in front of them with their headlights on and not to stop at the traffic lights. Tamale sat on the edge of the casket and let himself fall back onto the satin. Jimmy reached up to close the lid.

"So what do you want from me anyway?" Tamale said. "What do you want that you're being such a prick at my funeral?"

Jimmy looked down at him, death warmed over. "I want to know what happened in that garage," Jimmy said. "You never told me what really happened that night."

"What you afraid of?" he asked. "Maybe that you pulled the trigger?"

"Maybe," Jimmy said. "Yeah."

"And what good would knowing that do you now?" he asked.

"Closure," Jimmy said.

Jimmy thought Tamale tried to laugh. He couldn't tell. "You want closure?" Tamale said. "Pull down the lid."

"Tell me what happened," Jimmy said again.

"I'm dead!" Tamale said. "I can't tell you anything you don't already know. Close the fuckin' lid."

"Please, sir," a voice said. "Please, sir. Close the lid. It's not supposed to be open." It was one of the funeral guys. He looked distraught as he reached up and grabbed the edge.

Jimmy looked at Tamale. "Fuck you!" he said as the lid came down.

"Fuck you, too!" Jimmy heard Tamale's voice muffled through the wood.

All eyes in the room were on Jimmy. Kelly was smiling.

The funeral guy guided Jimmy away from the casket as the pallbearers surrounded it. Jimmy was supposed to be one of them, but the funeral guy held him back.

"It's always hard," the funeral guy said to Jimmy in his practiced funeral guy voice. "I understand the two of you knew each other a long time."

Jimmy looked at him. "Too long," he said. "We knew each other too long."

THE MAN WHO BUILT BOXES

This time it hit John Dodge on the morning of his forty-third birthday. He was heading into the giant hardware store that anchored the mall. It happened as he crossed the lot. Usually he didn't feel anything until he'd actually entered a store and the door closed behind him. He steadied himself by looking at one of the snow blowers lined up outside the entrance. He concentrated on the crank and gear assembly that rotated the chute. He liked gears. He liked how they meshed. He liked the physics of ratios. A larger gear turning a smaller one, the rate of the turn precisely linked to the diameter and the number of teeth. He counted the teeth, then took a couple of breaths. He steeled himself to go inside. He needed a miniature hinge for his latest project.

"Maybe you're agoraphobic," Sheila, the divorced waitress at the coffee shop, had observed when he started to tell her about these little moments. "It happens," she said, hijacking his story. "One day someone's just fine as can be and bam! They're filled with neuroses and phobias, can barely talk on the phone or step outside to pick up the paper and look for the cat." She finished their conversation with a confession that she'd been in successful therapy. Her testimony was suspect, however, when she also confessed that she quelled her panic each morning by circling her kitchen table six times before pouring her first cup of coffee.

It wasn't exactly panic John felt. It was more a sense of loss, a sense that he would never be happy. It wasn't unfamiliar. These little washes had come and gone most of his life. He remembered walking into another store in another mall during his doomed marriage. He was looking for a birthday present for his wife. As he entered a cheese emporium, he was slowed with a sadness that he'd forgotten something and would never quite remember what it was. That was almost ten years ago, months before he saw that marriage crumble under the weight of immaturity and discord.

The feeling was stronger today. He felt the energy draining from his body. He was standing by a display of toolboxes. They were familiar. Safe. Inviting. He reached out to touch one, hoping the cold steel would stop the deflation. He liked the red. He liked the silver and black edges of the drawer fronts. The handles. He reached out to try one. The smooth slide of the metal drawer. Ball bearings. A reassuring weight that spoke of quality construction and strength. He opened and closed several of the drawers, listening to the sound. Concentrating on the feel. Enjoying the slide.

"Can I help you?"

John looked up. A young lady with a lip piercing was standing above him wearing a Hinge World shirt and a name tag identifying her as Megan.

"You okay?"

John nodded. "Yeah," he said. "Just looking."

"That's fine," Megan said. "Just want to make sure everything is okay. You've been sitting there a while."

John realized he was on the floor, cross-legged in front of the display. The tool boxes were stacked above him, a wall of red metal and dozens of drawers.

"How long?" he asked.

Megan the Clerk shrugged. "Maybe twenty minutes."

"Oh," said John. He took a deep breath and started to stand. Megan grabbed his hand and helped him up.

"You sure you're okay?" she asked again. "Want some water or something?"

"I'm fine, thanks," John said. "Easy to lose track of the time, you know?"

"Yeah," said Megan. "Unless you're working extra hours because somebody didn't show for their shift."

John brushed off his jeans and smiled at the clerk. "I'm fine. Really."

"Okay," Megan said. "I'll be over in the tool section if you need anything."

"Great. Thanks."

John headed toward a sign that read, "Hinges." He found what he wanted, a pair of brass, half-inch, offset babies that could be used on the inside of a miniature door. He paid cash at the register and headed out to his truck. He drove home counting each of the traffic lights.

He pulled into his garage. It was a single bay off the kitchen of his little house. The garage was one of the things that appealed to him when he'd rented the place. It gave him a workspace. A wooden bench was set against the back wall, next to it a cabinetmaker's miter saw, and an antique, hand-operated drill press. The miter saw was a survivor of his divorce, something Stephanie had forgotten to put on her lawyer's inventory. The drill press was another story. It had belonged to his grandfather. Stephanie not only put it on the list but fought bitterly for it. In the end, it had cost him his car and the payments on hers.

"Oh, you're home."

John turned toward the open kitchen door. Early the Bird, a colorful Amazon parrot, was on the sill. It bobbed its head, then said, "Did you remember the milk?"

Early had been Stephanie's pet. She'd bought it when John and she first married, then spent hours teaching it domestic phrases.

"Did you remember the milk?" the bird repeated.

"Yeah, yeah, I got the milk, I got the milk," John said.

"Good John, good John," Early said and flew clumsily to the edge of the workbench.

On the center of the bench was John's latest project—a mahogany box about the size of a loaf of bread. The seven sides were not parallel, and the resultant shape was a geometric study with elegant, rounded edges and invisible joints. John lifted off the smallest side and set the new hinges in place. He worked with the precision of a jeweler, inserting the tiny brass screws in holes he had measured and drilled. When he was finished, he opened and closed the panel. A flawless fit.

John ran his fingers along one of the edges. Perfectly smooth. Except for a tiny burr near a corner. He took a piece of sandpaper, removed the offense, then rotated the box looking for other imperfections. The kitchen phone rang, a shrill call that made him grimace and made Early pace.

"It's your mother," a voice proclaimed through the answering machine. "You haven't called me."

"It's only been two days, Ma," John yelled at the machine.

"It's the anniversary, you know," the voice said.

"How could I forget with you harping about it?"

"We should visit. Bring flowers."

"You can bake a nice cake."

"I've baked a nice cake."

"And I should call you 'cause you'll be waiting."

"Call me. I'll be waiting."

"Hang up, Ma."

"Okay, I'm hanging up now."

She hung up. The answering machine beeped and reset.

"She's *your* mother not mine. *Your* mother not mine," Early the Bird chanted from his perch on the bench.

John took a swat at the parrot, but it jumped out of the way and flapped into the house.

John put the mahogany box in the center of the workbench and climbed the steps into his kitchen. It was a small room. Nineteen-fifties cabinetry. A lime green gas stove and refrigerator. Tiled counters. And 123 wooden boxes. They were everywhere—on the counters, above the cabinets, covering the table. Of the four chairs in the room, only one was empty.

The boxes were all sizes from a deck of cards to a case of beer, and all shapes from simple cubes and rectangles to uneven-sided forms that would challenge a mathematician. Some with parallel sides were stacked on one another. Others stood in crowded groupings like patrons in a bar. They were a mix of woods, the plainest made of finished ply, the more elegant crafted of exotic hardwoods and highly polished to reveal their complicated grains. The boxes spilled into the living room where another ninety-six covered the furniture and fought for space along the floor. Some of these were large. One was a dodecahedron with each of its twelve sides a perfect three-foot pentagon.

More boxes were in the hall and on the stairs that led to the second floor. A maple one matched the climb of the first four steps, a six-inch-wide series of rectangles joined at right angles that nestled perfectly against the risers and treads. In all, there were three hundred sixty-three boxes. Three hundred sixty-five if you counted the one on John's workbench, and the single, large, unfinished one that sat in the middle of his bedroom.

"Wipe your feet if you're going upstairs," Early admonished. "Wipe your feet."

John sighed and said the one thing that would shut the bird up. "Yes, dear."

Early waddled off, and John untied his boots and put them in the hall. He climbed the stairs and stood in the doorway of his bedroom looking at the largest of his projects. "The mothership," he called it. It was made of walnut, an expensive and finely-grained hardwood, polished to a magnificent finish. It was loosely shaped like a giant letter Z with ninety-degree angles. It was tipped forward so the top leading edge rested on the floor. The peaks were almost four feet high, and it was an easy six feet from end to end. The box was big. He'd have a hard time ever moving it out of the room.

John turned on a stereo that sat in the corner. Frank Sinatra played from speakers on the floor. John stood by the giant box and ran his hand over one smooth side. He felt along a bottom edge and triggered a release. A panel popped open revealing the interior. It was padded—a thick satin cushion covered the bottom and sides. A pillow was sewn onto one end. John knelt down and crawled inside. He lay on his back and rested his head on the pillow. The angles in the box matched those of his body like a custom recliner. It was a perfect fit. He reached over and closed the panel, then inhaled the solitude and muffled Sinatra.

He had almost fallen asleep when he heard the distant sound of his doorbell. He tried to ignore it, but it was persistent. Reluctantly, he opened the panel and crawled onto the hard floor. The bell was much louder.

Early the Bird was squawking in the doorway. "Why do *I* have to do everything? Why do *I* have to do everything?"

John took a swipe, but the bird jumped out of reach and trotted into the hall. The doorbell rang again. "I'm coming, I'm coming!" John yelled as he descended the stairs. His mother rapped on the glass, rattling it. He opened the door.

"I don't know why you just don't give me a key," his mother said. "It certainly would make life easier."

"Hello, Ma," John said.

"I called you," she said. "Didn't you get my message?"

"I just got home a few minutes ago."

"I made a cake," she said and held open a bag so he could see.

"It's great, Ma."

"You drive," she said. "I don't want to be late."

She brushed past him and headed into the garage. John closed his eyes, took a deep breath, and followed. Early the Bird bobbed on his perch in the kitchen. "*Your* mother not mine. *Your* mother not mine." John closed the kitchen door behind him. He climbed into the truck.

It took less than ten minutes to get to the cemetery. John's mother talked the whole time about her widowed neighbor's son.

He worked for the post office and was painting his mother's house on the weekends. A good son did things like that.

It was a large cemetery with three sections. One was very old. You could tell by the shape of the stones even without seeing the dates—thin stones, soft stones, most of which were no longer perpendicular. The lettering was hard to read. Time, rain, and wind had softened the edges. In another hundred years, none would be legible.

The monuments in the middle would weather better. They were newer and had more mass. Thick granite, highly polished with sharply carved names and dates.

John and his mother parked along a narrow roadway in the third section. Here the headstones were simple markers laid flat in the earth for the convenience of the groundskeepers. They were hidden from casual glance. John had always thought that these were the most vulnerable. Dirt filled the crevices of the letters and numbers, and sod crept over the edges of their faces. Left alone, these markers would readily slip below the surface.

The twins had died forty-three years ago that afternoon. James and Joseph Dodge. John brushed off the stone revealing the single date that marked the day of their birth and death. John's mother put down the bag and spread a blanket.

"I'm glad it's a nice afternoon," she said. "The twins would have liked that."

She settled onto the blanket with a weary sigh. John sat next to her. She looked at the gravestone for a long time, reaching over twice to touch it.

"I would be a grandmother now," she said. "Jimmy would have a little girl named after me. Joey would have two boys. It would be a grand birthday with the children running around."

John's mother pulled the bag toward her and took out the cake. She set it between them and put a single candle in the icing. Her hand was steady as she lit it. She blew out the match and started to sing the birthday song.

"Sing it with me, Johnny," she said.

Reluctantly, he did.

She rummaged for plastic cutlery, then cut a piece for each of them. "I waited so long for them to be born," she said. "I thought they'd come early, but they didn't."

"I know," said John. "You stayed in bed that whole last month."

"I stayed in bed that whole last month."

"Listening to Frank Sinatra records."

"Listening to Frank Sinatra records." She finished her cake. "You almost killed me too, you know."

"I know, Ma," John said.

"You were the biggest. Like a 'bully,' the doctor said. I was in labor for almost forty hours before you decided to come out."

"I know, Ma."

"The doctor said the twins never had a chance."

"My cord strangled them."

"Your cord strangled them."

She started to cry. Softly at first, then loud sobs.

"You know, Ma, they should have done a cesarean," he said. "It didn't have to happen that way."

"Oh, so now you're a doctor," she snapped. "When did you go to medical school? What do you know? You weren't there."

"But, Ma," John said. "I was."

He looked at her. She was facing away, wiping her eyes with a handkerchief. It would be easy. All he had to do was lean over.

It wouldn't take a minute. He would curl his fingers around her throat and squeeze. He took a breath and reached for her neck. His hand touched her shoulder. She shrugged it away and stood. She brushed crumbs off her dress and started to clear their litter.

John sat for a moment, then got up and walked to his truck. He watched his mother fold the blanket. She climbed into the passenger seat. Silently, they drove back to his house. She got in her car and left without a word.

John stood at his workbench to inspect his newest box one more time. It still needed a finish, but he gently picked it up and carried it inside.

Early the Bird was waiting in the kitchen. "Did you remember the milk? Did you remember the milk?"

"Yeah, yeah. I got the damn milk," John answered. The bird waddled away as John took off his shoes and wearily carried the mahogany box upstairs. He turned on the stereo, then climbed inside the mothership. He pulled the door shut and closed his eyes. He ran his fingers over the surface of the mahogany looking for imperfections. He felt none, and fell asleep to the muffled Sinatra.

MAX RYLAND
MEETS THE DEVIL

Max Ryland was a cocky son of a bitch. He was a good-looking guy just two years over thirty with a fervent sex life. He was at the top of his game and knew it. And that's why Max Ryland didn't recognize The Devil when he met her.

It was an office get-together, an end-of-the-quarter celebration. The executive search firm for which he worked had done well. It had been a great three months, better than great. Once again Max had been the alpha sales dog. Bonuses had been issued, and the gang was having a good time at a downtown tavern, a noisy mid-scale place with two large bars and a nice, professional clientele. During the week, most patrons came straight from the office still dressed to impress—suits and ties, skirts and heels. Thursdays and Fridays were the big nights. Lots of shopping. Desperate singles and not so singles looking to hook up, to score, to feel just a little more alive before an empty weekend and its following week of work.

Marcia Findley wasn't celebrating this Friday evening. She was too busy waitressing, hustling drinks, and ignoring the not-so-subtle gropes from the guys and several of the girls. She was a lady just trying to make a living. Max spotted her as she delivered an order across the room. She was attractive, no doubt of that. Short, dark hair, subtle makeup, a double piercing in one ear. Her red blouse was tighter than it needed to be. The V-neck boosted her cleavage and guaranteed more tips.

Max swirled the beer in the bottom of his glass and gestured toward Marcia. "I just decided on dessert," he said to his tablemate Scott.

Scott put down his drink. He raised his eyebrows, nodded his head, and said, "So be it."

Marcia, although Max didn't yet know her name, had a full tray. He could tell it was heavy. She expertly did the waitress dip, lowering the tray so she could unload while not allowing too easy a view down her blouse. Max tried to flag her, but she disappeared out the back. He pointed at Scott's drink.

"Ready for a refill?"

His friend drained the glass. "Sure."

Max straightened his tie and followed Marcia's path. He found her at the service bar putting in orders.

"Hi," he said as she checked notes on her pad.

"Hi," she answered and smiled without looking up. She had a dazzling smile, a little uneven. The right corner of her mouth was slightly higher than the left.

"I was trying to catch you. Got room for two more?'

"Sure," she said and flipped a page.

She had a pleasant perfume. Max inhaled, unconsciously leaning toward her. It was a natural, earthy smell. She looked up suddenly. Max was caught off guard by her eyes. Emerald green. Iridescent. He had never seen eyes like Marcia Findley's before. Sharp, clear, and with vertical irises like those of a cat.

"Wow," said Max, not quite realizing he had said it out loud.

"What?"

"Your eyes."

Her smile broadened. "Contacts," she said, raising her chin in a manner just short of defiance.

Max's heart was thumping. He held on to the edge of the bar. "So what would you like?"

Max realized he had stopped breathing. He inhaled.

She touched his hand. "You okay?"

He nodded. Her fingers were cold, but when she took them away, his hand felt warm. He felt warm. He thought he might be blushing.

"Drinks?"

"Yeah," he managed and gave her the order. "We're at the back table on the left."

"I know," she said and smiled again. "You were easy to spot."

Max staggered back to Scott.

"What's wrong?" Scott asked.

"I think I've been smitten." Max told him about her eyes.

"Be careful," said Scott. "She'll be able to hunt you in the dark."

Over the next hour, Max circulated among his coworkers, laughing, joking, and flirting with the company women. In the last month and a half, he had added three more of them to his life list. Sleeping with each had been a satisfying challenge. One was in a marriage she hadn't yet realized had failed. The second was a new mom who he caught off guard with his attention. The third had been his primary competition in the monthly numbers. That particular achievement had been especially gratifying as she'd made an open point of ignoring his charm and disparaging his sales prowess. It had taken a while to find the cracks in her armor, but when he did, he was pleased to discover her professional confidence and sure-footedness didn't make it into the bedroom. Each of these exploits was short-lived and ended in practiced confessions of "fear of friendship being lost" and the futility of office romances.

Rumors of the escapades made other female colleagues cautious but not unwilling. Tonight there were several overtures. Two unsolicited—subtle hints about being amenable to engage in more than just sales talk. A third, more overt, from Rita the VP of marketing, was the result of careful groundwork. During the previous weeks, he had been working her, targeting her with playful attention and frisky entendre. Tonight it was paying off. Rita approached him twice as he mingled in the crowded room, the second time pressing her lips against his ear and sharing a daiquiri-fueled fantasy about his glib tongue. This is where Max would normally play the advantage, but tonight he surprised himself as he sidestepped Rita's proposal. Tonight his attention was elsewhere.

Three more times during the evening, Max made a point of talking with Marcia, touching her arm, breathing in her scent. The last time, catching her in a quiet moment near the coatroom, he traced the letters on her name tag as he repeated them. When he withdrew his hand, he let his fingers brush the top of her breast.

Marcia shook her head and laughed. "I hope that's not your best move."

"It's not a move," Max said. "It's a question."

Marcia's feline pupils dilated. "Look," she said. "I'm really flattered. You're a good-looking guy, charming in your way, and I don't know why you'd be interested in a regular grade like me when you have all those high octane types in there." She touched his arm.

"It's been fun talking with you. And I hope you're a big tipper. But I'm a working gal with two kids at home."

"So that's a 'maybe'?"

Marcia smiled. "It's an 'I don't think so.'"

For a moment, Max lost heart, until she leaned forward to give him a kiss. Her scent was strong, enveloping. The kiss was light, hardly more than a gentle brush, but as her lips touched his, Max was hit with a blinding flash. He felt himself lying naked below her. She was straddling him, breathing hard. He gasped and opened his eyes. They were standing in the dim light near the restaurant coatroom.

"Oh my," she said, "you're sweating like a horse." She brushed a bead from his forehead. "Maybe I should have stopped serving you."

Max felt out of breath. "No," he said. "It's you." He reached toward her. She took his hands and gently squeezed them.

"It's the alcohol," she said.

He shook his head and closed his eyes. Again the flash exploded against him. He was on his back, Marcia naked, sitting on him, rhythmically pulling him into her. He strained to match her movements. She leaned forward lifting her weight. He followed with desperate thrusts. He felt her breath hot against his face as she pinned his arms with hers, and he raised his hips in magnificent climax.

For a moment Max felt as if he were in pieces, as if his body had simply come apart; a leg over there, a foot here, an arm there. He slowly opened his eyes. Marcia was standing in front of him. She started to laugh.

"Oh," she said, covering her mouth. "I'm sorry. But that was kind of weird."

"You felt it too?" he asked.

"I didn't feel anything," she said and raised her eyebrows. "But obviously you did." She pointed at the front of his pants. Max looked down. They were wet, soiled—evidence of his extraordinary experience. It took a moment for him to register embarrassment.

"Those are nice slacks," Marcia said. "You really should rinse them off in the men's room so they don't stain."

"She's right," a second voice said. It was Rita, arms crossed, standing near a coatrack. "Be a shame to lose such an expensive pair so cheaply. I'd help, Max, but I see you've gotten the waitstaff to service you."

Before he could respond, Rita turned and walked away. Marcia's eyes followed her down the short corridor.

"I have to get back to work," Marcia said and suddenly Max was abandoned, feeling naked among the coats and jackets.

"Jeez, man, where you been?" Scott asked when Max finally returned to their table. "You just missed the excitement, and what's with the pants?"

"Nothing," Max said and sat quickly to hide the evidence.

"Your new friend throw a drink at you?"

"Not exactly,"

"Oh. I get it." Scott chuckled. "You had dessert."

"It's hard to explain," Max said and changed the subject. "So what's the excitement I missed?"

"Rita's really drunk. She was dancing on the bar like a fool possessed. Started to strip. Got her bra off before a couple of her marketing gals came to the rescue. Gonna be hard for her to give anybody crap in the office after that." Scott chuckled again and started to count out bills for the tab. "Great boobs, though."

Max held his coat in front of him as they were leaving. Marcia was at the bar. She looked up as they passed. Her eyes flashed green as they caught the reflection of a light. Max could smell her across the room. He left Scott standing by the door and made a detour. Marcia was loading her tray.

"I want to see you again," he said.

"Why?" she asked, irises contracting.

"From the moment I first saw you—"

"Let's see," she said. "You couldn't take your eyes off me. You were really attracted to me. I remind you of an old girlfriend. Or maybe," she said with a little laugh, "it really was just the alcohol."

"No," Max said. "No. It's more than that. I can't explain it. But it's more than that."

"Oh, Max," she said, arranging the drinks on the tray. "I know you're attracted to me." She smiled again. "Your little problem attests to that."

"There's no little problem," he said. "That's never happened before."

"If you say so." Marcia lifted the tray.

"Please. Don't say no," Max said. "I do want to see you again. I want to get to know you."

Marcia rested the edge of the tray back on the bar. Her eyes dilated; the pupils looked almost normal. "Max, I'm a single mom. My life is pretty complicated."

She started to lift the tray again. He reached out and touched the back of her hand. It was hot. He leaned forward to kiss her. She put the tray between them.

"Max," she said, "I'm sorry, but I don't think it's a good idea."

"Give me a chance to show you otherwise." He gave her his best smile.

"Oh, Max." She took another deep breath. "I don't know."

"Just a chance to get to know you."

She searched his face. "Well," she said. "My car's in the shop. I'm off in an hour. I guess I could use a ride home if you'd like."

"Yes," Max said. "I'd like. I'd like it a lot."

"Just a ride home," she said.

"Just a ride home," he said.

"What was that all about?" Scott asked as he and Max walked across the parking lot.

"Working the close," Max said.

Scott laughed. "You're something else."

Max shrugged but suddenly wished he hadn't said it quite like that.

An hour later, Max was in his car across from the service entrance watching for Marcia among the departing employees. He enjoyed the anticipation. The first touch. The first kiss. The first caress. He closed his eyes. Had they already touched, kissed, caressed? The memory was confusing. He tried to evoke the reality of what had happened by the coatroom but couldn't sort it out.

He jumped when she touched his arm.

"Man, you scared me," he said, heart pounding.

"Sorry," she said, settling into the passenger seat. The pupils of her eyes were wide in the dim light. "I thought you might be asleep."

"After this evening, I may never sleep again," Max said and smiled. Her scent was strong, fecund. He started the engine, then leaned over to kiss her. She raised a hand between them.

"Please," she said. "Just a ride home."

He searched her face for ambivalence, then settled back behind the wheel.

"Which way?"

She gave him directions and he pulled onto the busy boulevard.

"How long you been working there?"

"Not long,"

"Good place?"

"I get to meet some very interesting people."

He glanced over at her. She was sitting sideways, back against the door, watching him. His eyes were drawn to her ample breasts. He felt a catch in his breath and looked away.

"That's a nice top," he said.

"Thank you."

"The red works well on you."

"It's a favorite," she said. "You don't think it's too revealing, do you?"

He swallowed. "Just right."

"It's such a balance, you know. If you show too much people think you're a slut."

He glanced again. He saw her topless against the door, arms crossed below her breasts—beautiful breasts, full breasts. He wanted to touch them, to feel them against his body.

"The road!" she said.

He looked up and swerved out of the path of an oncoming car.

"Maybe I should drive," Marcia said. "You've had a lot to drink."

"I'm fine," he said and gripped the wheel tightly.

He looked at her. She was fully clothed and facing forward, buckling her seatbelt, adjusting the strap across her chest.

In another block, she told him to turn, then directed him into a parking lot behind an apartment building.

"Thanks for the ride," she said. "I really appreciate it." She unfastened her seatbelt and reached for the door handle.

"Wait," said Max. "Just a minute." He started to undo his seatbelt, but she put her hand firmly on his, stopping him.

"Good night, Max." She leaned over and kissed him. This time it was more than a light brush. She pressed her mouth against his. It was hot. His lips burned. Her scent surrounded him, blanketed him, weighed him down. He felt the car accelerate. He tried to move, to hit the brake, but couldn't. She pulled away. The acceleration stopped as if they'd hit a wall. He felt the seatbelt clutch his chest. His breath left him.

"Max," Marcia said. "Breathe." He opened his eyes. Marcia was in front of him, cat eyes staring. "Breathe," she said again. It was as if he had forgotten how. "Inhale," she said. "Inhale." She put an open palm on his chest.

He gasped, pulling air into his lungs. He felt his body inflate.

"Exhale," she said.

He looked at her.

"It's okay. Breathe out."

He held the air for a moment longer, then blew it out, emptying his lungs. He inhaled again. Marcia's scent filled his body. He exhaled. He looked through the windshield expecting to see them against the side of her building. But the car hadn't moved.

"I don't think you should drive," Marcia said. "Maybe you should come up for a couple of minutes. I'll fix some coffee."

Max nodded.

It was a small place. A short hall opened into a living room/dining room. A playpen was across from a well-worn sofa. Toddler toys were scattered over the floor.

"Sorry about the mess," Marcia said. "My kids stay with my mom the nights I work. But I miss them, so I leave their toys out."

The apartment smelled like Marcia, a fertile mix of earthy perfume and motherhood.

"Have a seat," she said. "I'll heat some water."

The sofa was soft, past its prime with sunken cushions and arms that curved inward. He sank into it as the pillows engulfed him. He closed his eyes.

"Here," said Marcia.

He looked up. She was in front of him, coffee in hand. He tried to take it but had to strain against the pillows. With an effort, he freed one arm and reached for the cup.

"It's an old couch," she said, sitting on the opposite end facing him. "I've had it forever. Fits me perfectly, though." She wriggled into a comfortable spot.

She had changed her clothes. She was wearing shorts and a thin red top with shoulder straps. Her breasts were loose inside. She sipped her coffee. An end lamp threw her into silhouette. Max squinted against the light. He wanted to say something clever, something to impress her with his charm and worldliness, but his usual wit failed him. All he could manage was a plaintive, "Let me stay the night."

"Oh, I don't think you want to do that." She took another sip. "I'm a bit of an insomniac. I don't think you'd get much sleep."

"Who said anything about sleep?" Max said into the shadow, trying to see the features of her face. She stretched out her legs, resting a foot on his thigh. He took it with his free hand, caressing it. Her toes curled under his fingers. He felt his focus sharpen. He put down his cup, but she withdrew her foot.

"I need to ask you something," she said, sitting taller on the couch.

Max smiled. "Anything."

"Aren't you afraid?"

It was a strange question. No woman had ever asked him that before. "No," he said, shaking his head. "Should I be?"

"You've just met me," she said. "I know you've been around, but hasn't anyone ever warned you about strangers?"

"Are you offering me candy?"

"Three hours ago you didn't even know I existed," she said.

"And now I'm a believer," he said.

"Are you?" she asked. "A believer in what exactly? Fate?"

Max stopped the word before it left his lips. He wished he could see her face. "I'm a believer in you," he said, trying to manage his most sincere eye contact against her silhouette.

Marcia laughed. "Oh, Max. That's pretty corny." She put down her cup and leaned forward. "I knew you'd be there tonight," she said, lowering her voice.

The change in tone surprised him. "At the tavern?" he asked.

"I was waiting for you," she said.

"But you don't know me."

"But I do, Max. I know all about you," she said. "And the women."

"What women?"

"The one's you've successfully tempted."

Max took a deep breath. "I don't understand."

"I bet I even know more of their names than you do."

Max pushed away from her. He strained to see her face. "Have we met before?" he asked, then added tentatively, "Have we dated?"

"I love that euphemism," Marcia said. "It's so innocent."

Max tried to push farther away but was stopped by the arm of the couch, its curve wrapping around and holding him.

"I've watched you," Marcia said. "It's easy to see what drives you. How you look for the vulnerabilities. And speaking of which, Max, the way you've been bedding your way through the office has been very clever. You're managing to neutralize your competition without demoralizing any of the pretenders. Except for Rita, of course. After tonight, she'll be a problem, you know. Humiliating someone is not without humor, but embarrassment makes people dangerous."

"Who are you?" Max asked.

"I'm a stranger, Max." She leaned back. "Maybe you *should* be afraid."

Max's heart was thumping in his throat.

"And if you're afraid," she said, her voice assuming a husky growl, "you have two choices."

Max swallowed.

"You can stand up, walk out of here right now, and I promise you won't remember we ever met."

"Or what?"

"Or you can stay."

"And if I do?"

"I promise that you'll never forget."

Max felt his breath leave him. He struggled to pull it in. With it came the musky scent of the single mother of two. It filled him, inflated him. He took another breath, holding the scent as it permeated his lungs. He felt lightheaded as he moved across the couch toward her silhouette. There were no flashes this time, just a long, warm, welcoming kiss that invigorated and excited him. He opened his eyes. Marcia was naked and so was he.

"You're sweating again," she said.

He touched her face. His fingers tingled as he ran them across her lips, then let his hand slide down her neck, over her shoulder. He felt a surge of purpose when he took her breasts in his hands, a pleasant shock that caused him to gasp. Her breasts were warm and heavy. He squeezed and caressed them, feeling their splendid weight. As he leaned down to kiss them, his fingers started to burn. It was an odd sensation that traveled up his arms and into his chest. He tried to pull away but couldn't. He was stuck. He looked at his hands against her skin and saw the tips of his fingers melting. There was no pain, just a steady pull as his fingers and hands were drawn into her. He looked up. Marcia was smiling, eyes glowing. She leaned forward and kissed him. Her lips were hot, and he closed his eyes as he felt himself dissolve.

□ □ □

It was warm, humid. Tropical. The sun was bright, but it had been raining. Max had slept with the window open. A warm front had moved in and the heavy air had spawned a series of back-to-back thunderstorms. Max was sweating. He kicked off the damp sheet that covered his legs. The phone was ringing. He looked at his bedside clock. It was almost noon.

He fumbled for the handset. "Yeah?" he rasped into the mouthpiece.

"Max?" It was Scott. "Where the hell are you? You missed the sales meeting."

"What sales meeting? It's Saturday."

"It's Monday, you idiot. You need to get down here."

"Monday?"

"Yeah. Where you been? And my theory about Rita is inoperative.

She's bounced back from her little dance and is really pissed you're not here."

"I'm on my way," Max said and hung up.

He sat up. He felt heavy and moved in slow motion. His breathing was labored. His head ached, a throbbing that pulsed in his temple, sharpened by the light. He closed his eyes.

Monday? He sat on the edge of his bed. He tried to retrace the weekend. He had gone to the Friday office thing. He remembered making the rounds in the crowded bar, a blur of exuberance, a familiar excitement. Then he remembered Marcia. Eyes, breasts, a kiss outside the coatroom. He opened his eyes with a gasp. Marcia. Had he spent the whole weekend with her? The light was painful. He closed his eyes again. There were flashes of memory. Shards of images. Her red top. Her foot against his thigh. He remembered heat. Sweat. But it was all a tumble. A scattering of moments.

The throbbing in his head increased. Squinting, he dragged himself into the bathroom and grabbed a couple of pain killers, washing them down with water from the tap. He sat on the edge of the tub, gripping it, waiting for the medication to kick in. His breathing quickened. He closed his eyes trying for a clearer view of the weekend, wanting the pressure in his temple to subside. He tried to recall the actual sex. He strained to remember. A glimpse of his hands holding her breasts, then no more.

The throbbing lessened. He tried opening his eyes again. Still too sharp. He steadied his breathing, matching it to a rhythm drummed out by the pulsing in his head. Four beats in, four beats out. He stood carefully, then turned on the shower. He leaned against the wall and waited for the steam to rise. He adjusted the temperature and climbed in. He ducked under the spray, hands flat against the tile. He tilted his head to feel the sting against his face. He turned around and soaped his hands, rubbing them over his face, down his neck. He soaped under his arms, then lathered his chest and stomach. As he reached below his belly, he stopped breathing. He ran his slick hands inside the top of his thighs and up toward his navel. It was smooth and featureless. There was nothing there. No balls, no dick, not even the hint of pubic hair. The pain in his head increased as he pressed his fingers into his skin, feeling for life hidden underneath. It was a foreign territory, a landscape he did not recognize. He tried to cup himself, but there was nothing to hold.

Shaking, Max climbed out of the shower. He wrapped a towel around his waist and steadied himself against the sink. The throbbing in his temple was stronger. His breathing was fast and shallow. He faced the foggy mirror on the back of the door. Slowly he unwrapped the towel and let it fall to the floor. With a swipe of his hand he cleared a patch on the glass and felt himself deflate when he saw it wasn't just a mirage from his hangover. Below his belly, he was smooth as a doll, a flawless surface void of any male blemish. He covered himself with both hands and fell to his knees.

In a wave the weekend washed over him, sweeping him to the floor. A flood of sensation swirled around him. He fought to keep his head above the surface as he recalled the heat of being pulled into the woman he knew as Marcia, the soaring energy of his nerves and neurons moving among hers. But the recollection turned cold when he remembered trying to disengage, fighting to extricate himself. It had been agonizing to withdraw. And now, as Max curled on the floor of his bathroom, empty hands between his legs, he knew why.

ACCIDENT WITH A VIEW

Big Al Penniman saw it coming. It wasn't one of those slow motion things. He saw it in real time. He sat high in his SUV, two cars back in the right lane at the stoplight. It was a busy intersection with impatient drivers anxious for the green. The driver in the car in front of him, a low-profile Italian sports model, was a half-length back from the white line, revving the engine, playing the clutch, moving a couple of feet, then letting it roll back in an impatient repetition.

Impatient pedestrians, too. On the yellow, Big Al saw the middle-aged guy in a suit dash into the street from the left. The driver of the sports car, low to the ground, view blocked by a van, had no idea what was about to happen. But Big Al could see it coming and shouted an impotent warning against the windshield.

The timing was perfect. The light changed, and just as the car shot forward, the suit popped out from in front of the van.

The car caught the man at knee level, folding him onto the pavement. Even from inside the SUV, Big Al heard the crunch when the car slid onto him.

Several drivers raced away as if they'd not seen anything, too busy to be detained by police asking questions. Others sat suspended in motion, stunned. Several jumped out of their vehicles.

Despite himself, Big Al called 911; at least two other witnesses did the same. A woman knelt by the downed pedestrian, oblivious to the blood, talking at him, trying to get a response, feeling for a pulse. The way she touched him implied medical training, and when someone tried to pull him out from under the vehicle, she shouted, "No! Don't! He's caught. Wait."

In six minutes, first responders were on the scene. Several men helped raise the front of the car enough to let the EMTs drag the man free. They checked vitals and worked to revive him, but it was obvious to everyone that it was six and a half minutes too late. The guy in the suit had left the building.

The driver of the car, a curvy, thirty-something brunette in designer sunglasses and expensive jeans, stood by looking distraught. She shifted from one stiletto heel to the other, digging in her purse, fumbling for her ID.

Big Al gave a statement to a police sergeant, hoping the guy wouldn't check for outstandings in the process, especially after he asked Big Al to wait around until they were done. Another cop took pictures, holding the camera at arms' length as he snapped the damage to the victim and the car. Big Al made sure he turned away when the shot was at an angle that could have included him.

He smelled her before he heard her, a perfume he'd liked since high school. "Excuse me," she said. "You were behind me." It was the driver.

"Yeah," said Big Al.

"I didn't see him," she said.

"I know."

The woman was older than he'd thought. He could see the lines beneath the camouflage, and despite the sunglasses, could see also the wear and tear below her eyes. She was a dozen pounds heavy for her jeans and blouse. And the butterfly tattoo that peeked out from the top of one breast was sun damaged, faded. The mileage gave her a hard-earned attractiveness, and the familiar fragrance made Big Al smile.

"The light turned green," she said, "and just as I started, he was in front of me." She hugged herself. "Did you see him?" she asked.

"Not until it was too late."

A man interrupted, introducing himself to the woman as a rep from her insurance company. He pulled her away to huddle on the sidewalk, then came back and asked Big Al to repeat what he had already told the police.

When Big Al finished, he got back in his SUV and watched as the EMTs loaded the covered body onto a stretcher, then shoved it all into the back of the ambulance. A cop had the driver move her car to the curb. He motioned for Big Al to do the same. Soon it would all be over, traffic would resume, and Big Al hoped he would be free to go.

"Excuse me." It was the driver again, standing by his window.

"I wonder . . ." she said, "I wonder if you could give me a ride. I don't think I can drive right now. Not with blood on the car. I called a friend, but he didn't answer." She was clearly shaken.

"How far?"

"Just a couple of miles. Up Canyon Road," she said. "I'd be glad to pay you."

"Naw," said Big Al. "That's not necessary. I'll take you."

After the police asked their last few questions, he waited while she grabbed things from her car.

"Thank you," she said when she climbed in next to him, perfume wafting.

"Canyon Road, right?"

"Yes," she said, then burst into sobs. "I didn't see him. I didn't see him."

Big Al was caught off guard. "It's okay," he said. "It wasn't your fault. The guy was an eff-ing idiot trying to beat the light like that, just running into the street. It was stupid. Suicidal. It wasn't your fault."

"Thank you," she said, dabbing at the tears behind her sunglasses. "I'm Dolores del Rey. People call me Del."

"Big Al Penniman," he said. "Sorry it's such a shitty way to meet."

He turned onto Canyon Road. It was a winding drive with hairpin turns up into the hills above the city. When he first moved to the area ten years earlier, Big Al had fantasized about living up here. Some cliffside house with a magic view over the valley. A place where he could sit on his deck in the evening and look out over the city with a pair of binoculars or a telescope, maybe catch people with their shades up doing naughty things. But he quickly realized that was highly unlikely. He'd never be able to afford something in this zip code. Not while he was working for somebody else. Not while he was working as a forty-five-year-old, out of shape, trouble shooter for a cheap bastard who owned a trucking company. Not unless he could figure a better angle. No, the best he could wish for was a Sunday drive past these houses wondering how many necks the owners had stepped on to live here.

"It's right up ahead," Dolores said.

"Your name is familiar," he said.

"You're thinking of the movie actress Dolores del Rio."

Big Al nodded. "Maybe so."

"Lotta people tell me that. Born 1904. Birth name was Dolores Martínez Asúnsolo y López Negrete. She was popular in the silent film days. Then famous again for fucking Orson Welles before he was fat. Then for making it big as a movie star in Mexico. She died in the eighties, 1983. Turn in here."

"You know a lot about her."

"Figured I should know who people were mistaking me for."

A couple of dozen yards down the driveway a security gate blocked the way. Dolores pulled a remote from her purse. The gate swung open. The house was well hidden. A lot of vegetation, bushes, and trees disguising its shape. Flora was planted too close to let it be seen and too close to please any local fire marshal. Big Al couldn't estimate the size of the place. It was built at an angle, hanging on the side of a cliff, waiting for the right temblor or firestorm to set it free.

"Bet you have a great view from here," Big Al said.

"It's okay," she said. She started to open the door. "Thank you for the ride. I don't think I'm going to be able to drive for a while. I've never run over anybody before." She shuddered. "Jesus help me," she said and crossed herself. "That's not something I ever thought I'd be saying."

"Could I take a look?" Big Al asked.

"A look?"

"Yeah, you know, at the view."

She seemed puzzled.

He smiled. "I've always wondered what it would be like to live up here over the valley."

"Big Al, right?"

"Yeah."

"Big Al, I really appreciate you giving me a ride, but . . ."

"Yeah, that's okay," he nodded and waved his hand. "I'm sorry. It was not the right thing for me to ask."

Dolores del Rey raised her glasses and looked at him for a long moment.

"Big Al," she said. "I know it's only ten in the morning, but I really need a drink. Would you like to join me?"

The view was as good as Big Al imagined. The whole valley floor unfolded in front of him. Standing on the deck, it seemed they were suspended in air.

"It's like coming in for a landing at LAX," he said.

He looked over the edge. It was a good fifty-foot drop into rocks and vegetation and fifty feet below that, another house waiting to ski down the slope.

"Any wildlife up here? Mountain goats? Bears?"

"Bobcats and coyotes," she said. "And some big-ass owls. They hunt at night. You don't see any cute little puppies running around up here for long. Refill?"

She had opened a bottle of champagne. Big Al didn't recognize the label and figured it was probably one he couldn't afford. It was too fruity for his taste, but he'd be an asshole if he told her that. He held out his glass. She poured.

The main feature of the living room was a large telephone pole that rose from the center of the floor and disappeared through the vaulted ceiling. Big Al walked slowly around it.

"It kind of holds up this part of the house," she said. "Like a giant spike nailed into the rock."

"Doesn't seem like it would be strong enough," he said.

Dolores shrugged. "Do you think he was married?" she asked, sitting on a sofa near the windows.

"Who?"

"The man I ran over. Do you think he had kids?"

Big Al put his glass on the coffee table and sat across from her.

"I don't know," he said. "But you need to remember it wasn't your fault. You didn't even get a ticket. If you didn't get a ticket, it wasn't your fault. That's the rule."

"Will they call them?"

"Who?"

"The police. Will they call his family? Will they tell them on the phone, or will they go in person?"

"Dolores . . ."

"Del."

"Del, you got a bathroom I can use?"

Even the bathroom had a view. The spa tub was below a huge window. He could imagine soaking in here with a bottle of vodka, watching the sunset. Maybe somebody in the tub with him; some nice lady enjoying his company. Maybe somebody like this Dolores.

Standing at the john, a window above the toilet offered the same vista.

"Damn!" he said, realizing he had peed over the rim as he stared out the window. He wiped it up as best he could, flushed away the evidence, and washed his hands. Before he headed back to the living room, he checked the medicine cabinet above the sink. Old habit. A bottle of ibuprofen, a man's razor, and a prescription for a high-impact sedative made out to the lady. He emptied half of it into his hand, then put the bottle back. He stuffed the pills deep into his pocket.

She was still on the couch. She had served herself another glass of champagne. He noticed she was barefoot, then remembered she'd taken off her heels when they came in the front. "I hate this house," she said when he sat down.

"Hate it? Man, I'd loan out body parts to live in a place like this."

"That's because you don't have any history with it."

"You got a view to kill for. Privacy. Only thing missing is a pool."

"There *is* a pool."

"There is? I didn't see it."

"Off to the side. You have to go around the corner of the deck."

Big Al smiled. "Then you got everything."

"You married, Big Al?"

"Used to be."

"What happened?"

"We didn't want the same things."

Dolores emptied her glass. "That's a bullshit answer."

"It's the truth," he said. "She had some fairy tale of what marriage was supposed to be. I'd bust my ass working days and nights, and she'd spend all the money."

"So you pay alimony? Child support?"

"Just alimony." He smiled. "Every month. I write the check real slow. Sometimes I deliver it in person. Make her reach for it. One time I gave it to her in rolls of quarters." He laughed. Dolores didn't.

"She won then. You lost."

Big Al finished his drink and put the empty glass on the coffee table.

"How about you, Del. I don't see a ring on your finger."

She smiled. "Yeah, I won, too. Got this place. Got the car. Get a big check every month."

"Every guy's bad dream, huh?"

"I earned it," she said. "Besides, he can afford it."

"What's he do?"

She smiled. "A little of this, a little of that."

Big Al shifted on the couch. "You know, I probably should be going."

Dolores pulled her legs up under her. "Did that scare you?"

"Why should that scare me?"

"Well," she shrugged, "it kind of implies that he's not on the up. Could be somebody dangerous. Somebody you should be afraid of."

"Not too many people fall into that category," he said.

She stared at him. He stared right back.

"I've got another bottle chilled," she said. "One more glass?"

"Maybe another time."

"He's some computer hoo-ha," she said, moving off the couch. "Came up with some stupid-ass web thing four or five years ago that he sold for millions and millions."

She padded into the kitchen and opened the refrigerator. "So, nothing really illegal. Just very lucky. And very much full of himself. Aside from chasing tail, he's not done shit since." She handed Big Al the champagne.

He looked at the label. It was different from the other one, but he still didn't recognize it. He put it on the counter.

"It's a hundred something dollars a bottle," she said. "I have to say he has good taste in wine. I've been working my way through his collection."

"Come with the house?"

She replaced his question with her own. "Why you in such a hurry? Just one more glass?"

Big Al removed the foil and the cage. He grabbed the cork and twisted the bottle with his thumb on the top like he'd seen his boss do. Dolores got two fresh glasses and let him pour.

"A toast?" she asked.

He saw it wash across her face.

"To the pour bastard I killed this morning." She crossed herself. "May his family and God forgive me." They touched glasses and drank.

"How come," she said as they headed back toward the living room, "how come you got the morning off to come see the view? Don't you work?" She sat and patted the cushion next to her.

"Yeah, I work," he said as he sat.

"Doing what?"

"A little of this, a little of that," he said.

She laughed. "Fair enough."

He smiled as she took another sip, then closed her eyes and ran the cold glass across her forehead and the sides of her face. This close he could see how carefully she worked the eyeliner and mascara. And at the root of what he thought was natural brunette, he could see blond. Or gray.

"You ever buried someone, Big Al?"

"Me personally? Like dig the hole?"

"Like lose someone close to you. A loved one."

"Yeah, a couple a people."

"Like who?"

Big Al hesitated. "Like my old man. He died when I was playing high school ball. Dropped dead in the stands when I fumbled a play."

"Wow," she said. "Like you killed him."

Big Al shrugged. "Not really."

"'Not really'?" Dolores laughed again. "You don't sound too sure."

"I didn't kill him," Big Al said. "Chain smoking and being fifty pounds overweight killed him."

"You just helped it along," Dolores said. "Your mom still alive?"

"Yeah, up north, Fresno."

"You close?"

Big Al shook his head. "She married some asshole I never got along with."

"Who else you lose?"

"Friend of mine in a drunk driving accident."

"He the drinker or the drinkee?"

"She. It was a she."

"Interesting. Girlfriend?"

"Yeah. Sort of."

"Before or after your wife?"

Big Al smiled again. "During."

"I see," said Dolores. "How long ago?"

"Couple a years."

"You miss her?"

"Yeah, I guess."

"Every day?"

Dolores looked at him, waiting for an answer.

"I think about her a lot," he said, looking at the glass in his hand. "We had this fight. I called her something I shouldn't of. A particular female body part. She left pissed."

"Can't say I blame her," said Dolores. "I'd a left pissed, too. But not before kicking you in the pelotas."

Big Al took a drink, then asked, "So, who else you kill?"

"My daughter," Dolores answered. "In this very house."

Big Al felt the hair on his arms rise and realized he was holding his breath.

"She was six." Dolores grabbed a photo from the end table. "Jenny."

Big Al looked at it. A girl, dark hair with a big smile was standing in front of a gymnasium balance beam. A guy in sweats was next to her. The apparatus was set low, but still her head barely reached it.

"Cute kid," said Big Al. "Gymnastics."

"She loved it. Level six. Went three times a week. She liked being able to do things some of the bigger girls couldn't. Amazing how she could throw herself around. Like there was no gravity, you know? Like she could fly."

"Yeah," said Big Al, "I've seen it on TV." He handed the photo back. "Who's the guy, her coach?"

"My ex. The asshole. One of the few times he made it to a meet."

"He looks like a proud dad."

"He's not her dad," said Dolores. "I had her before I even knew the bastard."

"So what happened? You really kill her?"

Dolores looked at the photo, then gestured toward the deck. "She climbed onto that rail. Like a balance beam. Was standing, one foot perfect in front of the other, arms above her, ready to do a flip."

"Jesus. Why would she do something stupid like that?"

"Because," said Dolores, "I dared her."

□ □ □

Big Al wasn't always Big Al. Growing up in the San Joaquin Valley, he was a skinny kid, easy to pick on. Until the hormones hit. When he was thirteen, he grew six inches in a year and filled out more quickly than any of his classmates. He took advantage of it, too. Paid back each of the kids who had given him shit, one by one. He wasn't a good student but held his own on the football field. By the time he graduated, he had a job driving truck for one of the big produce companies. Good, steady work. And when there was a problem, especially one that might involve some troublesome driver, Big Al was the one his bosses asked to help fix it. He was good helping people see what was in their own best interest.

There wasn't much Big Al Penniman was afraid of. But he was afraid of this woman. There was something about this Dolores del Rey that made him wish he had dropped her off at the front gate and just gone on his way, just ignored her scent and gotten the fuck out of there.

Big Al leaned forward and put his glass on the table.

"I was drinking," she said. "My asshole husband hadn't come home all night, so I started early. I wanted to be ready when he showed up." She put her glass next to his. "Jenny was pestering me," Dolores said. "Wanted to show me something she'd been practicing. Was going to show me on the deck. But I dared her to do it on the beam."

Big Al looked at her. Her eyes were wide, large pupils looking at him.

"I want to show you something," she said, then got up and headed to the rail.

Big Al moved slowly but followed her.

"See that rock down there?" She pointed over the edge to the hillside below them.

"Lotsa rocks," said Big Al. "Which one?"

"By the scrub pine. To the left. Three, four feet. The one with the point. Bigger than the others."

"The brown one?"

"Yeah," she said. "That's the one she hit. The brown is from the blood."

A voice behind them said, "That's where I found them."

Big Al turned. It was the man from the photo.

"Jenny was dead. Dolores was next to her, trying to put her head back together."

Dolores started to cry. "They wouldn't fit," she said. "The insides. They wouldn't fit."

The man stood in the doorway. "Dolores." He put out his arms. "Come over here. Come back from the rail."

"I kept trying to put them back," cried Dolores, "but they wouldn't fit."

"Dolores," the man said again. "Please. Come here."

She looked at him, lost, then went to him. With an arm around her shoulders, he guided her off the deck. Inside the door, he turned her face to him. "Dolores, look at me." He held her chin in his hand. "Look at me." She started to resist, then stopped.

"I got your message," he said. "I saw the car, and I'm having the guys take it in to be cleaned."

"They wouldn't fit," she repeated.

"Listen to me," he said, giving her chin a shake. "I know what happened today. I spoke with the police. It wasn't your fault."

He helped her to the couch and sat next to her. He looked at Big Al. "You drove her home?"

"Yeah," said Big Al. "She didn't want to drive. Asked me for a lift."

The man looked at the empty glasses on the table and nodded. "Thanks," he said. "Maybe now you should go."

"Yeah," said Big Al. "Yeah, you're right. I gotta get going."

"I'm sorry," Dolores said to no one and started to cry again. "I'm so sorry."

"You know," said Big Al, "maybe it's not such a good idea for her to be out there driving."

The man almost laughed. "Yeah, maybe it's not such a good idea. Thanks for the advice."

"I'm just saying," said Big Al.

"Yeah," the man nodded. "You're just saying." He rocked Dolores while she cried. "You also saying you enjoyed drinking my wine and humoring my wife? Maybe that you thought you might get lucky? You dirtbags are all alike."

"Dirtbag?" Big Al took a step forward.

"Yeah. Dirtbag. What you gonna do? Beat the shit outta me?"

Dolores was sobbing into the man's shoulder.

Big Al realized he had clenched his fists. He could feel his fingernails digging into his palm. "Look," he said. "I didn't know about any of this." He gestured toward the deck. "Just trying to do a favor. I don't want any trouble."

"So, why don't you just do us another favor and get the fuck out?"

Big Al took a deep breath. He outweighed the shithead a good fifty pounds. Even out of shape, he could pick him up and toss him over the rail. Aim for that rock. Wouldn't take much.

The man wrapped his arms around Dolores.

"You know . . ." said Big Al, ". . . sure. No problem. You got your hands full."

Big Al closed the door behind him and walked across the drive. The man drove a new convertible. A red import worth three, four times what Big Al paid for the SUV. Big Al was tempted to drag a key across the hood and down the side. Instead, he climbed into his SUV and turned around in the driveway. The gate opened as he approached it.

"Fucking great view," he said as he drove onto the road, then without looking back headed toward the valley where he should have been two hours before.

GIRL IN A BOX

He was surprised by the box. It was larger than he expected. And heavier. When he came home from the office, it was sitting in his driveway. As soon as he tried to move it, he knew it would be a challenge. He could barely get it onto the dolly and into the garage.

"What was that?" she said, when he dropped an edge on the concrete.

"Hello?"

"That wasn't supposed to happen." The voice came from inside, muffled but easy to understand.

"Sorry," he said.

"You're supposed to be gentle. Didn't you read the book?"

Thirty-four-year-old Artemis Highlander sat on the floor. "I didn't see a book," he said.

"Did you even look?"

He had to admit he hadn't.

"And you think this is a good first impression?"

Artemis leaned back against the box. He hadn't thought this through.

"What's your name?" he asked.

"You should introduce yourself first," she said. "That's the polite thing. You still have time to salvage this."

"Hi," he said. "I'm Artemis. Should I describe myself?"

"Five ten," she said. "Brown eyes, dark hair, starting to gray around the edges. Cute smile. Generally outgoing. Good sense of humor. There's ten pounds you could lose and not miss, but you're in pretty good shape for a desk guy."

He was surprised. "I sound pretty likable."

"You are. I wouldn't have chosen you otherwise."

"Isn't this where you reciprocate?"

"Susan," she said.

"Hi, Susan. Pleasure to meet you."

"Are you sure?"

"Yes," he said. "Been looking forward to it."

A small opening appeared near his waist. "Give me your hand," she said.

He hesitated, then inserted it ready to shake. Instead, she turned it over. He could feel her on his palm looking for calluses, feeling his lifeline. Her fingers were strong.

"Nice hand," she said as she released him.

"Thanks," he said as she closed the door. He circled the box. "So how do I open this?"

"You don't," Susan said. "I do."

"Oh." Artemis nodded as if he understood. "So, open up."

She laughed. "You really should have read the book."

"Where is it?"

"Right here."

He looked for the opening but couldn't find it.

"May I have it?" he asked.

"Maybe later."

Artemis felt along the surface of the box, looking for seams.

"You didn't describe yourself," he said.

"What do you want to know the most?" she asked. "What I look like? Age? Personality? Interests? Political orientation?"

"All of the above," he said.

"Choose one."

"That's not fair."

"It's more than fair. Think of it as that first impression."

"Okay then. What do you look like?"

"Oh," she said. "I was hoping you'd be more original."

"Sorry."

"No matter."

"So, what do you look like?"

"Let me put it this way. I don't think you'll be disappointed."

"That's not very helpful," he said.

"Then give me your hand again." Another opening appeared. This one stretched from eye level to floor, just wide enough for him to reach through.

"Close your eyes." She took him by the wrist and raised his hand to her face. She held it as his fingers explored her eyes, nose, mouth. Even with his eyes closed, he could see her. Even features, high cheekbones, long eyelashes. Her hair was full, shoulder length. Smooth with a slight curl.

"Brunette?" he asked.

"With some highlights," she said.

As she moved his hand down her neck and across one shoulder, Artemis realized she was naked. He smiled as she guided him down her arm. It was firm, muscular. Smooth elbow, small wrist, and fingers almost dainty with soft skin and even nails. She took his hand in both of hers and brought it to the top of her chest and held it there. Then she drew it across her breast. He took a breath as he felt a nipple graze his palm. Her stomach was flat, firm. His fingers brushed over her navel. He got a glimpse of silky hair before she moved his hand to her hip. The bones were well-defined and highlighted a slim waist. Her bottom was a soft handful. She drew him down her leg, then released his hand and stepped away. He found himself reaching for her, fingers groping the air.

"Was that helpful?"

He nodded. "Yes." He was surprised at how visual it had been and how alert it made him feel.

"I'm glad," she said. "You need to go now, but maybe you'll come again. We can visit."

"I'd like that."

"Good," she said as she closed the door. "Good."

Over the next two days, Artemis visited the box each morning before he left for work and when he came home. Each time, he knocked and listened for her voice.

"Just a minute," she'd say. He'd step back as if waiting for someone to check him through a peephole. In a moment, an opening would appear, never in the same place. If it was high, he'd stand to talk with her. If it was low, he'd sit on the carpet he put at the base. He'd reach through the opening. She'd take his hand. He'd invite her out, but she'd decline, saying she had everything she needed right where she was. So they'd stay there, hold hands, and talk.

She'd prompt him about his work, about his day. She'd listen and empathize appropriately. It was only after the second visit he realized how adept she was at deflecting questions. She'd give a soft response, then steer him away, sometimes with as simple a tactic as letting his hand rest on her knee.

It was the third evening. He came home late. The natural light that filtered through his garage had faded. It was dark. He invited her out to see his place.

"I've already seen it," she said.

"You have?"

"While you were at work. I've wandered through several times. It's interesting. Reflects your personality."

"I'd love to see yours. May I come in?"

She ran a finger up his arm. "Oh, there's not much to see."

"But if you don't let me in, how can I kiss you?"

"Is that something you'd like?"

"Yes."

A door opened near his face. It gave him just enough room to lean through. She brushed her lips against his. He pulled away so he could touch her face. She held his palm against her cheek. He withdrew his arm so he could kiss her again. This time he tried to tempt her with his tongue. "I enjoyed it when you let me feel your body," he said in a whisper. "It's only fair if you want to feel mine."

"Is that something you want me to do?"

"Yes."

His heart was beating rapidly. She closed the door while he got undressed, kicking his clothes to the side. He stood naked in front of the box with an erection.

"I'm ready," he said. Another door opened.

"A little closer," she said. He stepped forward and felt her hand on his face. She ran her fingers through his hair. "Turn around."

With open palm she traversed his back and sides. As she reached his rear, he faced forward ready for her touch. His erection grazed her arm, but she moved her hand to his chest. He took her wrist as she had done with him. He started to draw her down his belly, but she twisted her hand free and placed it back on his chest. She leaned forward and kissed him. He tried to pull her to him, but the door was too narrow. She was wearing a robe. He felt it open and reached through it. He concentrated on the contours of her body. He squeezed her rear, then slid his hand to her crotch and pressed against her. He thought she opened her legs, but when he tried to wiggle a finger into her, she pulled away. He almost lost heart, but she dropped her robe, then turned and backed against him. Wordlessly she bent forward and let him enter, holding still against the edges of the door while he moved in and out, free hand pressing the small of her back. It was over too quickly. He stood with shaky legs, glad for the support of the box. She leaned forward, letting him slip out of her.

"Feel better now?" she asked in the dim light.

"Very. How about you?"

"I'm fine," she said. "Would you like to sit for a minute before you leave?"

He slid to the carpet, his arm against the door. "I'd like to stay," he said. "Lie beside you. Hold you." He reached inside. "Where are you?"

She took his hand.

They sat on opposite sides of the opening for several minutes. Finally, Susan leaned over and kissed him on the cheek. "Good night, Artemis."

"Good night, then," he said. "I'll see you in the morning." She closed the door. He heard the lock click.

The next morning when he came downstairs, he found his garage door open and the box gone. He sat on the carpet and watched the sun rise beyond the end of his driveway.

□   □   □

The bump jolted her awake. She'd been sleeping, dreaming about running through a meadow with arms outstretched. Running toward him in slow motion as he turned and opened his arms to sweep her in circles over the flowers. She launched herself the last few yards and just as they were about to embrace, he stepped aside and she fell to the ground with a thud.

"What was that?" she shouted as she sat up in her bed. The light was soft. The magic hour that photographers wait for twice a day.

"Hello?" he said, his voice muffled through the wall of doors.

She looked around, reminding herself of the surroundings. A night table was by her bed, a vase of flowers and a framed photo on it. A down comforter covered her feet. "You weren't supposed to do that."

"Sorry."

She sat on the edge of silk sheets and held her robe closed with a hand on her chest. "You're supposed to be gentle," she said. "Didn't you read the book?"

She heard him moving on the other side of the wall. "I didn't see a book," he said.

"Did you even look?" She sounded angrier than she intended.

"I guess I haven't."

"And you think this is a good first impression?"

Her heart was slowing. Her breathing steadying. She stood in front of the wall waiting for him to answer.

"What's your name?" he asked.

She shook her head. "You should introduce yourself first," she said. "That's the polite thing." She picked up the photo from the nightstand. "You still have time to salvage this."

"Hi," he said. "I'm Artemis. Should I describe myself?"

"Five ten," she said, looking at the photo. "Brown eyes, dark hair, starting to gray around the edges. Cute smile. Generally out-going. Good sense of humor. There's ten pounds you could lose and not miss, but you're in pretty good shape for a desk guy."

"I sound pretty likable."

She could hear the surprise in his voice.

"You are," she said as she put the photo back on the stand. "I wouldn't have chosen you otherwise." She opened her hand against the wall.

"Isn't this where you reciprocate?" he asked.

"Susan," she said. She could feel his heat. She closed her eyes and leaned the side of her face against the wall. It was warm.

"Hi, Susan. Pleasure to meet you."

"Are you sure?" She slid her hand down the wall in a caress.

"Yes," he said. "Been looking forward to it."

The tips of her fingers found a delicate knob. She hesitated, then opened a small door. Warmth rolled into the room. She flat-tened her back against the wall. Her mouth was dry.

"Give me your hand," she said. It appeared through the open-ing. She took it and turned it over. She pressed her fingers into his palm, feeling the textures of his skin and tracing his love line.

"Nice hand," she said as she released him.

"Thanks," he said.

As soon as he withdrew, she locked the door. She stayed with back against the wall, waiting for her breath to return to normal. She could hear him moving, exploring his side.

"So how do I open this?"

"You don't," Susan said. "I do."

"Oh," he said. "So, open up."

She shook her head and laughed. "You really should have read the book."

"Where is it?

"Right here." She reached to the floor and lifted a bound volume.

"May I have it?" he asked.

"Maybe later." She opened to a page with a downturned corner. There was a drawing of Artemis in front of a castle looking at a tower window.

She could hear his hands against the box, sweeping its surface, looking for clues.

"You didn't describe yourself," he said.

She placed the book next to the flowers. "What do you want to know the most? What I look like? Age? Personality? Interests? Political orientation?" She arranged the flowers so the bouquet was even.

"All of the above" he said.

"Choose one," she said.

"That's not fair."

"It's more than fair. Think of it as that first impression."

"Okay then," he said as she waited. "What do you look like?"

"Oh," she said. "I was hoping you'd be more original."

"Sorry."

She waved the apology away. "No matter."

"So, what do you look like?"

"Let me put it this way. I don't think you'll be disappointed."

"That's not very helpful."

She hesitated, then reached for another knob. "Then give me your hand again." She opened a door. This one stretched from eye level to floor, just wide enough for him to reach through. She let the robe slide off her shoulders to her feet.

"Close your eyes." She took his wrist and stepped in front of the opening. She raised his hand to her face. She held it as he explored her eyes, nose, mouth. He touched her hair, combing it with his fingers.

"Brunette?" he asked.

"With some highlights," she said, pleased with his perception.

She moved him slowly. Down her neck. Across one shoulder. She guided him down her arm, all the way to her fingers. She took his hand in both of hers and pressed it against her heart. She counted beats against his palm, then lowered him across a breast to her stomach. The tips of his fingers tickled her hair as she moved him to hip and buttocks. He squeezed her before she drew him down one leg. She let go and stepped away. She picked up her robe as he reached after her, fingers groping the air.

"Was that helpful?"

"Yes," he said.

"I'm glad," she said and wrapped the robe tightly. "You need to go now, but maybe you'll come again. We can visit."

"I'd like that," he said

"Good." She closed the door. "Good."

She sat on the edge of the bed, hugged herself, then started to cry.

The next day, while Artemis was at work, Susan opened a large door on her wall. It was big enough to walk through, but she just sat on the edge of her bed and looked into his garage. By noon, she had moved to the doorway. By 12:30 p.m., she was outside the box on the carpet Artemis had spread around its base. She kept one hand on the doorframe. It was an organized garage. A bicycle hung from the ceiling. Trash cans with tight lids were against the wall. Plastic containers for recycling were stacked near the entrance to the house.

She wondered what kind of car he drove and if he normally parked it inside. Briefly she let go of the doorframe but grabbed it when she felt dizzy. By 1:00 p.m., she had retreated inside, closing her door and checking that it was secure. An hour later, she found herself back at her wall, arms spread across its surface, the side of her face pressed against its coolness. Her hand caressed the doorknob. She dropped her robe to the floor. Twice she turned the knob until the latch clicked, then pulled back, letting the mechanism reset. By 2:30 p.m., she steeled herself, opened the door, and stepped through. She stood on the carpet naked and defiant. She looked back once, then raised her head and entered Artemis's house.

One by one she explored his rooms. She examined the furniture, the walls, the pictures on them. It was a mixed décor but thoughtfully arranged. Twice she stopped and picked up objects, one a wooden boat from a shelf in his study, another an art deco lamp from a table next to his sofa. She looked at each, feeling its weight. She closed her eyes and concentrated on the texture and surface.

She'd been in his house almost a half hour when she found herself outside his bedroom. She looked through the door. It was a plain bed, neatly made, covered with a handmade quilt. Homey. Not something she would have chosen. But soft. Inviting. There was a bureau, two night tables, and a television. A DVD was on the quilt. She stretched to see the title. It was a Triple X with warnings of "adult content" printed across the breasts of the woman on the label. A porn magazine was beneath it. Susan took a step into the room. She slid the magazine toward her. She flipped through the pages, looking for signs of favorite ladies. The centerfold was wrinkled. A vacant, young thing bent over with hands on knees as a faceless man entered her from behind. The girl in the photo was smiling over her shoulder into the camera. The man was lost in himself, one hand on the center of her back as he arched into her. Susan studied the picture, then mimicked the pose next to Artemis's bed.

She heard a car in the driveway. She replaced the magazine and ran through the hall, barely making it out of the house before Artemis unlocked his front door. She wrapped her robe around her and leaned back against her wall, panting for breath. She checked her locks as she listened to him approach on the other side. He came to the box and knocked.

"Just a minute," she said. She looked through a peephole and saw him waiting for inspection. She sat on the floor and chose a knob. She opened a door. He sat across from her, the wall between, and reached through. She took his hand.

"Would you like to come out?" he asked.

She squeezed his fingers. "Not right now," she said.

"Do you need anything?"

"Thank you. No. I've got everything I need."

She encouraged him to talk about his day. She listened and prompted. Several times he asked her questions. She answered vaguely and distracted him by caressing his arm and placing his palm on her knee.

The next day, Artemis stopped by in the morning and again after work. It was late. The natural light that filtered through his garage had faded. It was dark. He invited her to see his house.

"I've already seen it," she said.

"You have?"

"While you were at work. I've wandered through several times. It's interesting. Reflects your personality." That afternoon there had been a different magazine on the bed. A different wrinkled center photo.

"I'd love to see yours," he said. "May I come in?"

She ran a finger up his arm. "Oh, there's not much to see."

"But if you don't let me in, how can I kiss you?"

His question surprised her. She almost let go of his hand. "Is that something you'd like?

"Yes."

She took a deep breath, and in a single movement, opened a door by his face. It was just large enough for him to lean through into the darkness. She moved toward him, letting him touch his lips to hers. A gentle kiss. He pulled back and reached in to caress her face. She held his palm against her cheek. He withdrew his arm so he could kiss her again. This time she felt his tongue.

He stopped and whispered. "I enjoyed it when you let me feel your body. It's only fair if you want to feel mine."

"Is that something you want me to do?"

"Yes."

Before she could say no, she heard him undressing. She closed the door and locked it. She stood with palms against it. She could see him on the other side, motionless, waiting.

"I'm ready," he said.

She chose a door wide enough to let her arm move freely, but too narrow for him to enter. He was standing just out of reach.

"A little closer," she said. He stepped forward. She touched his cheek, then ran her fingers through his hair. "Turn around."

With open palm she traversed his back and sides. As she reached the bottom of his spine, he faced forward. He had an erection. It grazed her arm. She lifted her hand to his heart. He took her wrist and drew her down his belly. She twisted free and placed her hand back on his chest, holding him away. She leaned forward and kissed him in consolation. He tried to embrace her, but the door was too narrow. His tongue caressed hers. She let her robe fall open. He reached beneath it, squeezed her rear, then moved his hand between her legs. She parted enough for him to wiggle a finger into her and felt herself moisten. She pictured the photo from his bedroom, dropped the robe, and turned around. She bent over, hands on knees, and backed against the doorway. It hurt when he entered. She heard him gasp. She pushed backward against the frame, bracing herself as he moved in and out. His hand pressed heavily on the small of her back. She distracted herself by digging her nails into the muscles above her knees. As soon as he was finished, she pulled away and grabbed her robe. She put it on and held it tightly around her.

"Feel better now?" she asked.

Artemis was leaning against the doorframe. "Very," he said. "How about you?"

"I'm fine," she said. He reached toward her. She dodged his hand. "Would you like to sit for a minute before you leave?"

He slid to the carpet, his arm against the frame.

"I'd like to stay," he said. "Lie beside you. Hold you." He reached through the opening, palm upward, fingers spread. "Where are you?"

She knelt across from him and took his hand.

They sat opposite each other for several minutes. Finally Susan leaned over and kissed him on the cheek. "Good night, Artemis."

"Good night, then," he said. "I'll see you in the morning."

As she closed the door and locked it, she felt the robe wet against her. She took it off, wiped herself, and tossed it away. She reached for a clean one that hung next to her bed. She put it on and cinched it. She checked the locks on her wall, then sat on the silk sheets. She rearranged the flowers, got up, and checked the locks again. Only after she knew all was secure did she lie down. She'd let herself sleep several hours, then would leave before he was awake. If she didn't, he'd expect her to keep opening the doors.

WOMAN WITH A GUN

DJ remembered the exact moment it struck him. He had TiVo-ed a popular cable series—an involved, high-tech procedural where they almost always got the perp before the end credits. It was the last shot. A public park in the warm Miami sun. The lieutenant and his two detectives had just completed their successful apprehension and turned the killer over to the uniforms. They walked in slow motion toward the camera as lyrics from some almost-familiar artist added the requisite ironic counterpoint. One of the detectives, a leggy blonde with a left-brained penchant for scientific detail, was in the lead. She wore slacks, blouse, sensible flats, and a sidearm that could bring down a bear. DJ watched the shot two or three times. It hadn't occurred to him before that moment how alluring a woman with a gun could be.

He supposed that's why he felt the heat when he first met the lady cop. She had just come off duty and slid onto a bar stool next to her partner. The bar was half a block from the station. Cops stopping in after shift wasn't unusual. The place had its regulars, but in the week and a half he'd worked there, he hadn't seen her before. She had an attractive edge. Thirty and change. Short hair, red, just covering her ears. Shape only partially disguised by the uniform. Sergeant stripes on the sleeve and a name tag that said

Smith. Dressed some other way, he doubted he'd peg her for someone on the job.

"You're new in here," she said, voice rougher than he'd guessed.

"Not so new," he replied. "Just clean up well."

It was lame, but it got him half a smile. She ordered a shot and a beer and watched him closely while he got them.

"Something familiar about you," she said. "We met before?"

"I don't think so," he said.

"You sure about that?" she asked, eyes squinting.

He put the drinks in front of her. "I'd remember," he said, giving her his most serious look.

"Yeah," she said, matching his expression. "You would."

Basketball was on the tube. March Madness. Her partner was into the game. He was a younger guy with a much older belly. When a timeout was called, he turned into a talker. He said they'd had some chase action earlier that evening. Caught some kid forcibly borrowing money from a customer at an ATM. Asshole didn't know the place was staked and made a run for it when their black-and-white appeared.

DJ listened as he wiped the bar. The sergeant nursed her beer and watched his reactions.

"Short chase and long paperwork," the partner said as he turned back to the TV, "but there's always that rush."

The sergeant tilted her bottle toward DJ. "How about you, new guy?" she asked. "You like that rush?"

Her partner cheered a classic hook from a young star rumored to be going pro before graduating.

"I like a good game," DJ said.

"Yeah," she said. "Me too."

When she headed out for a smoke, DJ enjoyed watching her walk. She had that cop gait that came from hauling the gear on her belt, and the cop habit of brushing her hand over her gun to make sure it was still there.

"That your truck out back?" she asked when she returned.

"Which one?"

"The red beater with the cap."

"Yeah," he said. "It's got a little mileage."

"Like you?"

She paid her tab, said good night to her partner, and left.

"Dakota," she said when she came in the second time.

"North or south?"

"Like I haven't heard that before," she said. "My name. Dakota. I'm officially introducing myself." She stuck out her hand. "Most people call me Cody." Her handshake was firm.

"DJ," he said, pointing at his name tag.

"David James," she said.

A good guess, DJ thought.

"The usual?" he asked. She nodded and he put out the drinks for her and her partner. The partner was already into the game.

"Lots of paper work today?" DJ asked.

"Slow," she said. "Makes the shift seem longer." She downed the shot and took a sip of beer. "I hate it when there's nothing happening."

"Sometimes you have to make your own action," he said, feeling it was the right amount of barkeep banter to juice the conversation.

She smiled.

Cody didn't show the third night. The fourth night she came

late. The Final Four game was almost over.

"Honey, you're home," DJ said as she and her partner took their usual stools. "Missed you."

"Of course you did," she said.

A half hour later DJ was getting ice from the freezer down the hall near the kitchen. She surprised him in the dim light.

"Been trying to think why you seem familiar," she said, thumbs hooked in her belt. She had her cop stance. Feet apart, protecting her center of balance.

"I get that a lot," DJ said. "Usually it's a good thing." He closed the freezer. As he turned, she stopped him with a hand on his chest.

"You wanna know something funny?" she asked. "Some guys like being frisked."

"That so," he said.

"Yeah," she said and spun him against the wall. He dropped the ice. "Spread 'em," she said, hand on the back of his collar. As he flattened his palms against the wall, she kicked his feet apart. "You know, something told me you knew the position. You carrying?"

"Carrying what?"

"Don't get smart," she said. "I don't want any surprises. Any sharp objects? Anything gonna stick me if I check your pockets?"

"No," he said.

She patted down the sides of his body, then up one leg, a hand inside his thigh. When she got to his crotch, she squeezed him through his pants. "I think you lied about carrying," she said and pushed her other hand into his pocket.

"Everything okay, Sarge?" a voice came down the hall.

Cody pulled her hands back. "Yeah, Wilson. Everything's okay."

DJ felt the rush as he headed back to the bar. His hands were shaking as he put the ice in the cooler. Cody watched him. When he looked up, she was gone, bills on the bar to cover her tab. Her partner said nothing, but left a few minutes later.

The little hall incident rattled DJ. He had a hard time concentrating the rest of the evening. He was glad it was slow. His boss closed the kitchen and sent him home. He headed out back and unlocked his truck

"I ran your plates," a voice said behind him. DJ turned. It was Cody. She held a cigarette, leaning against a big SUV parked next to him.

"Find anything interesting?"

She took a long drag, then flicked the butt past him. "A couple of things," she said. "Like you did a little time upstate."

She was out of uniform now, jeans and a sweater just loose enough to cover her sidearm. DJ opened the door.

"Need a favor," she said and gestured toward the SUV. "I locked myself out."

"Don't you have some cop trick to get inside?" DJ asked.

"Yeah. A brick through the window. How about a lift home?"

She looked uncomfortable riding in the passenger seat. She gave terse directions, guiding him across town one turn at a time.

"You're single," she said.

"Now," he said. "Married a couple of years. Didn't work out."

"Seldom does," she said. "Seeing anyone?"

He shook his head.

"Pull over there." She pointed to a space by an apartment building. It was an older building, rundown. She sat for a moment looking up at the windows. Most were dark. She turned toward him. "Why don't you come up for a minute?"

He hesitated. "I don't think that's a good idea."

"Relax," she said. "I'm off duty. Besides, you got some better place to be?"

He looked at her. She smiled. He turned off the engine and followed her to the entrance. She took several loose keys from her pocket. The first one didn't fit. "New keys," she said and tried a second. It let them into the lobby. The elevator wasn't working. They walked up two flights. The stairwell was musty.

"My roommate's asleep," she said. "Gets up early. We'll have to be quiet." Cody put a key in the lock. It fit, but she had to jiggle it to make it turn. She looked up and down the hall, then put her finger across her lips and let them in. The room was dim. She shut the door without turning on a light. She kissed him hard enough to push his back against the wall.

She grabbed his elbow. "Down the hall," she whispered.

"How much you want me to resist?" he asked, keeping his voice low.

"Up to you," she said as she pushed him into a bedroom. Light from the street filtered through the curtains. "Get undressed."

"You first," he said and sat on the edge of the bed.

"Resisting?"

"Not yet."

She pulled off her sweater, then slid her gun under the pillow. She unbuckled her jeans as he unbuttoned his shirt. In a moment their clothes were on the floor, and they were on the bed. She straddled him, holding his hands flat against the spread. As she leaned down to kiss him, the room light snapped on. In one move she snatched her gun from beneath the pillow and rolled onto her back aiming at a figure in the doorway.

"What the fuck?" It was a man, startled, in his underwear. A big guy. Tattoos on both arms. "What the fuck you doing?" He took a step toward them. Cody straightened her arm, aiming at his chest.

"On the floor!" she shouted. He hesitated. She raised her aim to his head. "Now!"

He was breathing hard, glaring at her. DJ thought he would grab for the weapon.

"Fuck," he said, then got on his knees.

"Face down!" she ordered as she climbed off the bed. She grabbed the cuffs from her jeans and with one hand locked his wrists behind him. She leaned over him, pressing the gun into his shoulder. "You need to lie there and not move," she said. "Got it?"

"Fuck you," he said.

She pressed harder into his shoulder. "Got it?"

"Yeah, yeah. I got it."

"Good." She dragged a blanket over him and turned to DJ. "Get dressed," she said as she pulled on her jeans. "We're not staying."

"What's going on?" DJ asked as they raced down the stairs. "That your roommate?"

"Gimme your keys," she said as they ran to the truck.

She jumped behind the wheel, gun between them on the seat. Before he could fasten his seatbelt, she had them swerving into traffic and running a light at the end of the block. DJ held onto the grab bar on the dash.

"How's your heart rate?" she asked. "Thumping?"

DJ nodded. It was.

She ducked them into an alley and stopped halfway down. She shut off the engine and pulled him toward her. His head was spinning. In a moment he was on top of her, one hand reaching beneath her sweater. She pushed him away.

"Feeling the rush?" she asked.

He couldn't respond.

She sat them up on the seat. "The rush." She shoved her hand between his thighs. "Oh yeah," she said. "You're feeling it."

He leaned toward her, but she pulled back.

"I was hoping we could get a little more into it back there before being interrupted," she said.

"That guy," DJ said. "You live with him?"

"Hardly," she said. "He's some loser I busted a couple of months ago."

"What's he doing in your apartment?"

Cody laughed. "It's not my apartment," she said. "It's his. When we processed him, I made copies of his keys," she said. "Visited his place a couple of times when he's been out. Wanted to know where the light switches were. Where he slept. If he kept any weapons on the premises."

"It's not your apartment?"

She shook her head. "I wouldn't live in that dump."

"I don't get it," DJ said.

"The rush, David James. The rush." She leaned back against the door and lit a cigarette. She stretched her legs onto his lap and blew the smoke across the cab. "Admit it," she said. "You like the adrenaline."

DJ reached over and with shaky hands took the cigarette from her. He took a drag and handed it back.

She inhaled deeply and stared at him. "Yeah, a few more minutes would have been really nice."

DJ looked up and down the alley. "You know," he said, be easy to finish what we started." He slid a hand along her thigh.

Cody laughed again. "Yeah, we could," she said. "But what's the fun in that." She reached into her jeans. "I got two other keys." She offered them to him.

DJ took them. They were warm from her pocket. And sharp. Whoever made them hadn't buffed the edges. He cut a finger.

"Blood on the first date," she said. "Like being a virgin in high school."

"Me or you?"

"You're no virgin," she said, passing him the cigarette. "You did time for breaking and entering. I could smell it on you that first evening in the bar."

"It's not something I'm proud of," he said.

"How long you in?"

"Year and a half. Got out early."

"Clean now?"

"Yeah."

"Parole?"

"Six more months."

She nodded. "Boring, ain't it."

He took one last drag, then cracked the window and flicked the butt into the alley. "Sometimes," he said.

"Not like slipping into someone's bedroom," she said, "going through their shit. You ever do it when they were home?"

"Couple of times," he said.

She smiled. "You know, I bet we could be really quiet," she said. She reached over and unfastened his belt. He squirmed under her fingers expecting her to touch him as she unzipped his pants.

But she didn't. "We could slip in, get undressed," she said as she brushed her lips against his ear. "Do it without making a noise." She kissed him. He leaned into her. She pulled back and put her hand flat on his chest holding him away. "Think you could do that?" she asked. "Do me without making a sound?"

DJ knew she could feel his heart pounding under her palm.

"I could act like I was arresting you. Search you. Find things you're hiding. Make you convince me not to take you in. All without raising alarm."

"And what if we did raise alarm?" His voice cracked.

She picked up her gun from the seat. "I'm a trained professional," she said, holding it in her palm. "I'm good at convincing people to think twice before doing something stupid."

"Like now?"

She laughed and put the gun back on the seat as she straightened herself behind the wheel.

"Why don't you conceal that thing," she said, gesturing toward his lap. "Give me something to look for later."

DJ tucked himself back into his pants.

"It's only a couple of blocks north of here," she said as she started the engine. "We could be in and out, so to speak, before they know it." She smiled at her joke.

"That is a bad idea," he said.

"Yeah," she said. "You're right. It is." She put the truck in gear and patted his thigh. "We should just head south, back to the parking lot. I'll unlock my car; we'll forget this whole thing ever happened."

At the end of the alley, she stopped before turning into the street. She lit another cigarette, then passed it to him.

"So," she said. "North or south?"

He took a deep drag, then blew the smoke toward the windshield. It curled down the glass and along the dash. She reached out her hand.

"It's a very bad idea," he said as he slid the cigarette between her fingers. "Very bad."

WHEN IT'S OVER

Cliff Wayland was jealous. Jealous of characters he'd find in novels or watch on TV. Envious even of what he'd see in magazine ads, the most recent one for carpet with an anonymous couple lying on their living room floor, legs entwined. Simple touch. Simple acknowledgment. A wordless moment saying so much.

That evening at a dinner party across town, Cliff watched friends sitting on a sofa across from him and Brooke. So effortlessly, the woman reached over and touched her husband's shoulder. The man turned toward her and smiled. Her hand slipped to his arm and squeezed it before she looked away to finish her story, to make a point in the conversation. Later, she rested her head on his shoulder. Only for a moment as her arm draped across his lap, hand resting on his thigh.

It was hard for Cliff to watch, but he did while he continued his part in the conversation. He laughed and joked and forced the energy that made his company pleasant. He did it cleverly so no one noticed that his wife never touched him.

When it was time to leave, Brooke hugged the couple. Her arms reached out and surrounded each of them and held them for a long moment. And for part of that moment, the woman, looking at him over his wife's shoulder, saw behind Cliff's face when his smile dissolved.

THE MAN WHO BUILT BOXES

His wife took her coat, thanked their hosts for a wonderful evening, led Cliff through the door, and walked ahead of him down the driveway in silence.

"It was a nice evening," said Cliff as they drove away.

She responded so quietly he had to lean toward her and ask her to repeat herself. "It was fine," she said, then turned and watched the darkness through her window. Cliff reached toward her and rested his hand on her leg, giving it a gentle squeeze.

She crossed her arms and said, "Please don't." When he retreated, she brushed her leg with the palm of one hand, smoothing imaginary wrinkles on her slacks.

"We should invite them over," Cliff suggested. She said something he could not hear, but he didn't ask her to repeat it.

When the job was finished, he'd sleep. He'd shut off his phone and get out of bed only when his bladder insisted. He knew from experience it would take three days—three days to feel halfway normal. But for now, forty-one-year-old Cliff Wayland only had the luxury of anticipation while he worked pretty much around the clock. The irony for him was that he didn't really give a damn about the outcome. His client could go to hell for all he cared and probably would. He was a hired gun paid to clean up a town; paid to ignore the facts or the ethics; paid at an exorbitant rate that a client wouldn't question until long after the checks cleared. That was the nature of the business. They didn't care how much it cost until the crisis was over.

The morning news conference was less than ten minutes long. The CEO had little to report. She began with heartfelt sadness for the family, then read the prepared statement and took a few questions from the assembled reporters. All of the questions were anticipated, and all of them she had practiced with Cliff the hour before. Most of her responses were vague assurances that the company was searching for the answers and would share them when available. She looked appropriately glum and gave good eye contact. And she managed to be the most sincere when she said, "Once we understand how this happened, we want to make sure that it can never, ever happen again, that no family will ever have to deal with something like this again."

All in all, it went well. Enough to assuage temporarily those present and to buy more time to distance the company from primary responsibility.

By Friday, the story had disappeared from the cable news previews. Cliff knew most of that was a matter of luck, which depended on what else was happening in the news. Something new and shiny that would grab the attention of the media and become the problem for one of his compatriots in another PR firm. He'd keep the war room open through the weekend, however, just in case the episode reignited on the Sunday talk shows. Besides, it would be another seventy-two billable hours for each of the three members of his team.

"Did she die?" Cliff's daughter Emily asked when he called home.

"Yes, sweetie, she did."

"Oh, Daddy, that's so sad. Why didn't the company just pay for the operation?"

"It wasn't their fault."

"But, Daddy, who cares? The thing wasn't working right."

For a moment Cliff thought about trying to explain how the actual medical device manufactured by his client wasn't the problem. It was the software. And the software was developed and programmed by a different company. But he was tired and knew his thirteen-year-old wouldn't cut him the slack. The fact that the device had been installed in the chest cavity of a seven-year-old would trump any case he'd try to make to a teenager.

"I liked her picture," said Emily.

It was a photo of the little girl from her previous birthday. She was sitting cross-legged holding her month-old puppy. It was the backdrop photo all of the news outlets were using when they updated the story and its aftermath. A pretty child with her beloved pet. Couldn't have been worse.

"I liked it too," Cliff said. "Is Mommy home?"

"Not yet. She had some meeting."

He tried Brooke's cell. Twice. It went to voice mail.

Cliff had been married to Brooke Peters for almost fourteen years, since just before Emily was born. The pregnancy had been unexpected and ill-timed. Brooke was finishing law school, and Cliff had just started a new job with a marketing firm. Neither of them had been ready to make a commitment to each other, much less take on the responsibility of a baby. It seemed a foregone conclusion that Brooke would terminate the pregnancy quickly before it could seriously complicate anything. But Brooke hesitated, and the window closed. They convinced themselves it was a good thing, and for many of the subsequent years it had been.

"We're over the hump," Cliff said after Brooke's recorded voice invited him to leave a message. "I'm going to crash at the hotel, then catch a flight out of here in the morning. Should be home by noon." There was a time when Cliff ended his Brooke calls with, "Love you," but now, hesitating, he just added, "See you soon."

□ □ □

Brooke Peters tried to ignore the vibrating of the phone. She'd forgotten to turn it off, and it clattered on the hotel lamp stand. The man lying on top of her didn't seem to notice. He was close to finishing and too focused to care. With a final thrust he lifted his head and moaned as if in pain. She had hoped for a roar, or a vulgar curse, or even a laugh, and was disappointed when he finished so lamely. He collapsed on her. Brooke had a hard time catching her breath under his weight. She pushed him off. He rolled onto his back, leaving a slimy trail across her thigh.

"That was great!" he said.

"Good for you," she said as she reached for the phone. She had feared it was her daughter calling, but it had only been Cliff.

"I'm sorry you can't stay," the man said.

"Yeah, me, too. It would have been nice to finish."

The point of her remark failed to pierce his fog. She sat on the edge of the bed and wiped herself with the sheet. She grabbed her clothes from the floor and disappeared into the bathroom where she washed off the rest of her disappointment with a plush hand towel. With luck, the loser would be asleep by the time she flushed the toilet and scurried out. He'd certainly had enough to drink. Maybe he wouldn't even remember what had happened. No, she thought. He'd remember. When she was writhing under him trying to gain traction, it had made a definite impression.

She had told her daughter she'd be home by 9:00 p.m., and it was almost 9:30 p.m. She texted Emily that the meeting was over, and she'd be home soon. She was rewarded with an almost immediate, *K.*

"I'm glad I didn't skip that last panel session," the guy said when Brooke came out of the bathroom, dressed as if she were late for a flight. "I wouldn't have met you." He was still naked on the bed, limp and worthless. "Thanks for escaping with me to the bar."

"Well, thanks for the drink." She gathered up her bag and checked for her keys.

"I'm based in Seattle, but I travel a lot," he said as she headed for the door. "How about you? Maybe we could meet up again."

"Oh, I doubt that would work," she said and ducked into the hall. She pulled the door closed behind her, then added, "Asshole."

Alone in the elevator she leaned back, closed her eyes, and took a deep breath. She was thirty-nine years old, a month and a half short of her "big-oh." She was a successful professional, the mother of a teen, and a wife. And she was clinically depressed.

She felt the beginnings of a migraine. The door opened. She thought it was the lobby, but she'd forgotten to press the button and had ridden up instead of down. Two men and a woman got on, all laughing and all wearing name badges for the conference the hotel was hosting. It was a popular venue, one of several in town that could accommodate a thousand-plus attendees—a thousand-plus strangers among whom she could be anyone except herself.

Brooke kept track of the conferences at each of the major downtown hotels, choosing those that pulled an international crowd. She would read a little about whatever industry was hosting so she could seem knowledgeable when mingling in the hallways outside of the meeting rooms. She would go in the late afternoon near the end of a conference when attendees were tired and looking for reasons not to sit through one more session. Organizers would no longer be religiously checking name badges. It was easy to be charming with a stranger, especially one a long way from home like Seattle. She knew the questions to ask as she feigned interest in his work. She knew when to touch his arm if he said something he thought was humorous. And she knew how to close: "Well, I for one am ready for a drink," she'd say.

To which he would almost always respond, "May I join you?"

They would find their way into one of the crowded hotel bars where she'd let him buy her a glass or two of wine. She'd encourage his flirt and let him realize he might have a chance. She'd boost his excitement when they'd step into an elevator. She liked her little games and the challenge of the chase; it sometimes lifted the cloud. If the car was empty, she'd reluctantly let him kiss her. If it was full, they'd stand in the front facing the door, and she'd let her hand brush his thigh, then press into his crotch. She would predict how confident he'd be in bed by how much he fumbled unlocking the room. This evening, Seattle had dropped the door card and had to try twice before the lock clicked. The rest of their session had been equally disappointing.

This time the elevator stopped at the crowded lobby. Brooke threaded her way to the exit, then down the street to where she'd parked. It would be a twenty-minute drive once she made her way onto the parkway. It would have been easier if she had left her car in the commuter lot that morning. But when she stayed late in the city, she liked escaping into the privacy of her own space. She could crank up the music and cheat a cigarette as she watched the lights of oncoming traffic. Sometimes her little liaisons left her elated, other times ambivalent. The worst, however, were the times like tonight when she felt it was all just a waste of time, not just the evening's chase, but the whole damn race. At the finish line, what would be the point? This was when the oncoming headlights were inviting, when it would be so easy to play the moth, drift just a little to the left of the center line and ride the lights to the end of the tunnel.

Cliff flipped through the movie titles on the screen. Sometimes he'd worry about the accountants seeing the in-room charges on the receipts. Although the titles would never be listed, it was easy to tell the adult fare from the merely violent and misogynistic by the higher cost. The people in accounting might get a chuckle or two, figuring one of the VPs was entertaining himself, but Cliff's real fear was that they'd figure out how alone he was. That they'd see desperation in how he'd put a line through the charges on his hotel receipt and subtract them from the total. Sometimes it bothered him, but as he explored the descriptions and images of ladies on the hotel screen menu, each of them looking him in the eyes, he forgot the accountants and enjoyed feeling the fleeting confidence of being a healthy male.

He and Brooke had tried couples therapy the year before. She was reluctant but relented when he agreed that it would be a person of her choosing. It took a month for her to tell him they had an appointment and only three visits to realize the man Brooke had chosen was not an ally. At first, Dr. Zorbian seemed sympathetic, but during that third session, Cliff felt blindsided when Zorbian nodded and said Cliff needed to accept that this part of his relationship with Brooke was over. That it was okay for him to mourn the loss of physical intimacy. Mourn the loss? What the fuck was he talking about? Cliff didn't want to mourn the loss. He wanted the man to tell his wife what was wrong with her and fix it. He remembered looking over at Brooke and seeing her smile. She visited Zorbian for another month, but without him.

Cliff chose a video with two women and toys. He welcomed the rush of hormones as the ladies invaded each other. He rode it to a quick climax, then fell asleep while they continued without him.

Brooke came into the kitchen from the garage. Emily was in the family room texting friends and watching TV. The dog, a three-year-old chocolate lab named Coco, bounded into the room carrying his favorite toy. He dropped it at Brooke's feet, then pushed his nose into her crotch, sniffing the evidence of her evening. "No, Coco," she said, trying to move his head away as Emily came through the door.

"Hi, Mom."

"Sorry I'm so late, honey. The meeting was much longer than I thought." Brooke tried to distract the dog by opening the food cabinet and fumbling for a treat. "Is your homework done? Did you eat?"

"Yes and yes," Emily said.

Brooke led Coco to his bowl with a dog biscuit. "When's the last time he was out?"

"About a half hour ago."

"Well, go take your shower and get ready for bed. Tomorrow's a school day."

"No, it's not," said Emily. "Tomorrow's Saturday."

"Oh," said Brooke.

"Did you talk with Daddy?" asked Emily. "He was going to call you."

"He called while I was in my meeting," said Brooke. "I haven't listened to his message yet."

"He's coming home tomorrow," said Emily. "Maybe we could have a family fun night."

"I don't know, honey. I need to be in my office tomorrow. Maybe we can do something on Sunday."

"That's what you always say, but we don't. You always have to go to the office."

"I'm sorry, Emily. But that's my job. That's what I get paid for."

Emily said nothing but stomped up the stairs and slammed the bathroom door.

"Shit!" Brooke dug in her purse for the prescription. She shook two pills into her hand, washed them down with a swig of wine from an open bottle in the refrigerator, then for good measure she added a third.

She heard the shower start and headed up the stairs. Coco followed. She stripped in her bathroom and grabbed her underwear from the dog when he tried to steal it from the floor. She pushed him out and closed the door. The panties were stained, a damp souvenir from Seattle. She buried them in the hamper and climbed into the shower. She made the water hot and soaped away the last of the dismal evening.

Cliff would be home the next day, but she didn't know when. Maybe he left the time on her voice mail. She would plan her day around his arrival, making sure she wasn't there when he returned, then it would be easy to feign a business dinner, and with any luck she could stay away until he was asleep. If he woke, she'd plead fatigue and slip into the guest room. Brooke ducked her head under the spray. She'd sleep in the guest room anyway. That's what she'd been doing for weeks now. When he traveled, she'd temporarily reclaim her space in the master bedroom; the mattress was better and it was easier getting dressed in the morning. But when he was home, she always found an excuse to collapse on the bed down the hall. He didn't even question it anymore. Maybe his period of mourning was over. Besides, it wouldn't be long before she'd be out of the house altogether. It wouldn't be long before she would be in her own apartment.

The wake-up call startled him. He thanked the caller before realizing it was a recording. The television was still on, the movie in a loop. He wondered how many times the ladies had violated each other since he'd fallen asleep. In the light of day, they looked tired as if waiting for him to turn off the tube so they could collect their pay and go home. What he'd seen as lusty enthusiasm the evening before now seemed mechanical with each of the players sneaking peeks at the camera operator for direction and moving the hair of the other so it wouldn't obstruct a view. He groped for the remote and turned it off so they could rest.

He checked his cell for messages. Nothing from his crisis team. Nothing from Brooke. Just one short text from Emily the night before: *Dad, mom's b-n a *itch!*

He texted her back: *Hang in sweetie. I b home soon.*

Emily carried her phone everywhere. It took less than a minute to hear back: *Better this morn. Still zzz.*

U still sleeping or mom?

Mom

Have b'fast and take dog out. Heading to airport.

K

He took a shower and packed.

The shuttle to the airport was slower than he'd hoped. The driver promised he'd be there in plenty of time to check in but hadn't told him they'd be stopping at three other hotels first. It gave Cliff time to contact his team. Nothing had exploded overnight, and it looked like it would be quiet over the weekend. The funeral two days earlier for the young girl victimized by his client seemed to have been the apex. As he'd hoped, other news had displaced the public's interest. But if it threatened to reignite, the team he left behind could take care of things until he flew back in.

At the airport he got another text from Emily: *Mommy wants 2 no when flite gets in.*

He felt like texting back: *Then mommy should ask me herself.* But better judgment prevailed, and he sent Emily the ETA.

It was going to be a bumpy ride. It was raining, and while they were sitting on the tarmac getting ready to taxi away from the gate, the pilot gave a short rundown of the weather and the expected turbulence. It was a small plane, a turbo prop. Some of his colleagues didn't like the smaller planes—too noisy and unsteady. Cliff, however, preferred them. The high decibel level of the engines precluded casual conversation and guaranteed solitude. Another thing he liked about the commuter flights was that they flew so much closer to the ground. He could look out the window and follow local and neighborhood roads. He could look into yards, count cars in the driveways, and enjoy the patterns of the streets and cul-de-sacs. Once he flew from Washington, DC to New Haven, Connecticut. It was before 9/11, and when they flew over New York, they were only a few thousand feet above the tops of the iconic buildings. It was late in the evening, and he remembered looking down on the lights and recognizing the World Trade Center passing below him.

The only thing that made him uncomfortable on these commuter flights was when he had to sit in a row next to one of the propellers. He liked seeing the engines come alive and loved the sound of them revving to full RPM. But he had this secret fear that the propeller blades would shake loose and slash their way through the cabin wall. Once the plane started rolling down the runway, however, he relaxed, closed his eyes, and enjoyed the vibrations and acceleration.

They lifted off and Cliff noticed the yaw as soon as the wheels left the ground. They were moving forward, but because of the wind, the body of the plane crabbed several degrees off center. As they climbed into the rain, the buffeting began. It was a bumpy road. Cliff pulled his lap belt tighter and put on the noise-canceling headphones Emily had given him for Father's Day. He plugged them into his phone and scrolled for music that he could crank and overpower the effects of the storm. He would be home in less than two hours. He wondered if Brooke would be there or manage her escape before he pulled into the driveway.

Cliff would be home in less than two hours. It was earlier than Brooke had hoped. She'd wanted to pack up the last of the files from her home office. Over the previous two weeks, she'd been stealing a half hour here and there to sequester things she'd need in the apartment. She was subtle in her packing. When Emily asked about the boxes, Brooke practiced the line she had planned for Cliff—that she was putting stuff in storage in the attic. It would work as long as no one climbed the stairs to look. Brooke had been moving things a box at a time in the trunk of her car. She had decided early on not to take any furnishings or small appliances. Their disappearance would be too obvious. She'd been buying minimal furniture online and had greased the building super to accept the deliveries. The subterfuge was one of the few things that lifted her spirits. It was the secrecy of it. Like her hotel outings.

But today called for a change in plans. With Cliff returning before noon, she wouldn't be able to do much at home. Instead, she'd take her briefcase and have Emily report that she'd gone to her office. She would then head to the apartment to set up what she could.

Although the adolescent Emily had moments of adult maturity and clarity, this morning she was being a teenager. She was answering questions with single words and angry body language. At least there weren't any door slams. Emily had gotten up before her. When Brooke came downstairs, her daughter was in the family room, earbuds plugged in, and texting. Coco was working on a piece of rawhide on the floor.

"Has the dog been out?"

"Yes," Emily said and turned away to prevent any accidental eye contact.

"Has he been fed?"

"Yes!"

Brooke went for the coffee.

She hadn't slept well and was feeling rancid. The headache had kept her awake much of the night. She'd gotten up twice to take something for it. Anything. The pain killers from her doctor were taking too long to work, so she'd supplemented them with OTC analgesics. An hour later she'd downed a couple of prescription anti-inflammatories that Cliff used for his back. Things hadn't mixed well, and she woke up on the floor next to the bed, puke on the hardwood. She had taken more pain meds before heading downstairs.

She was surprised how much her hands shook when she poured a cup from the coffee maker. It was hot but bitter, dregs from the day before. She leaned against the counter and waited for the caffeine. Sometimes it would soften the edge. But this morning, she needed it to clear the fog. Maybe she should lie down, sleep another hour. She could still escape before Cliff got home. No, she couldn't take the chance. She carried the cup with both hands back upstairs.

The bedroom still smelled of vomit. She had wiped it up, but the scent lingered and made her gag. She felt the coffee coming up and lost it in the sink. She was sweating and dizzy. Her hands were numb, and her legs gave out before she could make it to the bed.

It was a rough flight that ended in a rough landing. Even the lone steward looked rattled. Taxiing to the terminal, the fellow sounded shaky as he reminded them to stay seated until they came to a full stop. Halfway through the flight they'd had a sudden drop, a good five hundred feet. Laptops and iPads flew. All in the cabin had been strapped in, so no one was thrown, but the screams were loud enough to be heard above the straining engines. The rest of the flight Cliff was fierce in his grip on the armrests.

Several people applauded when they touched down. Everyone was quiet now. Cliff had peed on himself during the fall. But he hadn't been the only one whose body had betrayed him. You could smell it in the cabin—bathroom odors that mixed with sweat and fear. All wanted the door to open and free them, and when it did, those aboard moved quickly to grab their bags and exit. The pilots did not appear. The cockpit stayed closed. The steward did his best to assure the departing passengers that all was well, but when Cliff passed, he could smell that the man's bladder had failed him too.

Cliff changed his underwear in the handicapped stall of a men's room, then walked the concourse to the main terminal and escape. It was still raining as he wheeled his bag to the parking lot.

"Daddy, you stink!" Emily said when she ran to greet him in the kitchen.

"I'm glad to see you, too, sweetie."

"No, really," said Emily. "You smell like a wino."

He found Brooke on the floor in the upstairs hallway. When he called her name, she didn't respond. He knelt beside her. He felt a fear forming in his stomach and throat. He shook her shoulder. "Brooke!" He shook it again.

With a groan she pulled her knees to her chest.

"Brooke," he said. "You okay?"

She shrugged his hand away and asked, "What time is it?"

"Almost noon."

"I have to get out of here before Cliff gets home," she said, her voice a quiet slur.

"Brooke, it's me, Cliff."

She opened her eyes and looked at him. "What time is it?" she asked again.

"Why do you have to leave?" he asked.

She rolled onto her back spread eagle. She was wearing an old favorite t-shirt, one that advertised a bar that had long closed. It had been washed so many times it barely reached her navel. In a different time and place he would have moved between her legs and stretched himself over her, pushing up the shirt and kissing her breasts before laying his bare chest against hers. He put his hand on her stomach. She didn't push it away.

"My tongue is stuck," she said. "I can feel it, but I can't talk."

"You're talking okay," said Cliff. "I can understand you fine."

"Cliff?"

"Yes."

"What are you doing here?"

"I'm home," he said. "I just got in from the airport."

She opened her eyes again.

"Why do you need to leave?" he asked again.

"I need to be at my apartment before you get home."

"Your apartment?"

"Yes."

Cliff lay next to her, careful not to let their bodies touch. "I know about your apartment."

Brooke lay silent next to him.

"Brooke?"

"How?"

"They did a credit check. I got an e-mail when the credit bureau flagged it."

"Oh."

"When were you going to tell me?"

She rolled onto her side away from him, resting her head on her arms. "I don't know."

"Does Emily know?"

"No."

"That's pretty shitty, don't you think? Just moving out."

She was slow to respond. "It's the only way I know how to do it."

Cliff stared at the ceiling. He hadn't realized he'd done such a lousy job painting the hall burgundy two years before. The line where the wall and ceiling met was uneven, sloppy. He should fix that. Maybe he'd paint it white again. The burgundy darkened the space. He'd like to brighten it up. He took a deep breath. "When did you stop loving me?" he asked. "When was it over?"

"That's unfair," Brooke answered.

Cliff started to laugh. "Unfair? You're furnishing a secret love nest and I'm being unfair?"

"It's not a love nest," she said. "I just need to be alone. I can't do this anymore."

"Do what?" he asked.

"Be with you."

"Brooke, you haven't been with me for years."

"I don't know when it was over," she said. "It just stopped. I don't know why. It just did. A long time ago."

Cliff looked down the hall. Emily was sitting on the top step listening. She looked at Cliff, then got up and ran to her room.

Brooke sat up in a panic. "Emily!" she called and was answered with the slam of the door. Brooke got up and stumbled to it. It was locked. "Emily!"

"Go away!" Emily yelled. "Go away! You don't want to be here! I hate you! Get out! Get out! Get out!"

"Emily!" Brooke shouted and banged her fist against the door. "Unlock this now!"

When there was no answer, Brooke turned to Cliff. He was standing at the top of the stairs, hand on the rail. He shook his head and left her alone in the hall.

□ □ □

"Daddy," said Emily, "when is Mommy coming home?"

They were driving back to the house from Emily's school. Cliff had picked her up after her class had returned from a field trip to a downtown museum. It had been a month and a half since Brooke had thrown her clothes into the back of her car and driven away.

"Sweetie, I don't know."

"I saw her today," said Emily.

Cliff looked over. "Oh?"

"She didn't see me, though."

"Where was she?"

"When we were getting on the bus to come back, she was going into the building across the street."

"The hotel."

"I suppose."

"Did you text her?"

"She said she had a meeting and would call me later."

"You know," said Cliff, "Mommy said you could stay at her apartment anytime you want."

"But I don't like it there. I have to sleep on the couch. I'd rather stay home."

They pulled into the driveway.

"Daddy?"

"Yes?"

Emily reached across the seat and took his hand. "I don't think she's ever coming back."

Cliff looked at her.

"I'm sorry, Daddy."

He felt the tears behind his eyes. He nodded.

"Thank you, sweetie."

"It sucks, you know," Emily said.

"Yes," said Cliff. "It does."

ANTONIO'S YARD

Antonio Enzo Marino was aware of the shift when he woke up a half hour early. It was almost palatable as he moved his coated tongue over his teeth.

"Shit!"

He had lived in Italy almost thirty years, a citizen by blood for twenty, but still swore in English. It helped to explain why his neighbors often referred to him as "The American."

He swung his legs over the side of the bed and looked out the window. The morning sun rose over the hills across the valley. He pushed opened the glass and stuck his head into the humid air. At the end of the yard, just a dozen meters in front of him, the storage shed that held a lawnmower, two bags of potting soil, and a sorry collection of gardening tools was gone. Not a trace. As if it had been plucked from the earth by a giant hand. But Antonio knew better. It had fallen over the edge.

"Shit!"

He pulled on his jeans, jammed his feet into his shoes, and went outside, letting the screen door smack behind him.

It was warm. That summer there hadn't been a full week where it had gotten below 80° F, even in the middle of the night. He stopped halfway across the yard and approached the edge ginger-ly. There was a single paving stone partially buried in the dirt, its surface angled away. It was one of the four he had sunk into the ground with his own bare hands just two years before as a foundation for the shed. The other three were gone, along with the soil that had held them in place—along with the whole back end of his yard. Antonio dropped to the grass on his hands and knees, and crawled the last few feet, feeling the ground ahead of him as if he moved in the dark.

He flattened himself and looked over the brink. Far below him, a good 100 feet, amid the rock and rubble, were the remnants of his shed, alongside that of his neighbor's moped.

The soil under his right hand gave way, dissolving into the air. Antonio pushed himself away from the precipice, then rolled over two or three times, putting distance between him and the unstable ground. He ended on his back, looking up at his house, bright in the morning sun—two stories of medieval stone fitted precisely in place by masons who could not see the future.

Antonio sat on the stoop. Almost thirty years he had lived here, half a planet removed from those who had once known him. And for almost thirty years, he had watched the ancient village around him, built on a fragile plateau of volcanic tuff, crumble inch by inch into the valley below. He and his neighbors, few in number, clung to a fantasy that some miraculous force would shore up the perimeter of their village, would stop the inevitable. But he knew it wouldn't happen. There was no miraculous force. There was no natural force. There was no man-made force. There was only the tick of time.

Adelina had been gone two years now. To the day. Antonio was surprised it could have been that long. They had been together close to two decades. Everyone assumed they had been married, and neither of them dispelled the assumption, which Antonio had been careful to create. He had met her during a month-long holiday in Menorca, and when he returned, there seemed no reason for her not to come with him. She was single, finishing an apprenticeship with a local winemaker, and ready to move on. She had buried both her parents the year before, and the liaisons she'd had with several of the local married men left her knowing there was no future for her there.

To quiet the wagging tongues of neighbors, Antonio had implied that they'd known each other from "earlier times," finally gotten married, and that the holiday had been a honeymoon. Since then, they had lived quietly, Adelina working for a vintner in a nearby town, Antonio for a succession of local businesses as an illustrator. They hadn't had children, although for a short period had tried. Adelina had been the only child of parents who themselves had been only children. It was a small family, unusual among those in the village north of Rome in which she had grown up, and she would be the only one to carry forward the family genes. Antonio had been indifferent, but Adelina fantasized about surrounding themselves with a noisy brood. It never happened. Antonio knew it was one of the many grudges they secretly held against each other—she, that he had never impregnated her, and he, that she pushed him too hard to compensate for her loss of family.

Antonio had also known that she kept a lover for several of those last years. And perhaps the biggest grudge she held was that Antonio had never confronted her.

He was surprised when he'd gotten the phone call that she had been killed in an accident on her way home one afternoon, surprised that he didn't feel a greater loss. She had been riding her bicycle, hit by a tour bus making a blind turn too fast to stop. He played the role of bereaved spouse well, letting neighbors and those with whom he worked bring food and comfort. He had her cremated and spread the ashes in the small garden she had kept along the edge of the yard, the part that early that morning disappeared into the valley below. The part that no longer existed.

In the months after her death, it had been easy to use the bereavement as an excuse to politely defer well-intended introductions to unmarried sisters and daughters. They understood it was too soon for him to leave Adelina behind, even when he spent an unexpected night or two with several of the local women. And now, with the collapse of another piece of his yard, Adelina had left *him* behind, completely. She had freed herself from the bonds of the rich black earth that Antonio had brought home on his scooter, bucket by bucket, to build the garden that she loved to till, and into which she would ultimately disappear.

He had never really loved Adelina. He had realized that less than a month after she had moved in with him. During the weeks in Menorca, it was easy to mistake the frenzy of a holiday romance for something with permanence. Perhaps he should have questioned a future then, but the rest of the pieces seemed to fit together so well that it was easy to ignore the obvious. He liked her. He enjoyed her company. The sex was good. They had some interests in common. But he had never truly loved her. Not the way he remembered loving Brenda Ann Beinecke.

The trunk was a classic steamer, made in the late 1800s from oak slats with iron end caps and a brass lock. Antonio had found it years before in the back of a shop in Soriano nel Cimino two hours north of Rome. The shop owner had intended to restore it but had never quite gotten around to it, so when Antonio, in his rudimentary Italian, showed interest and made an offer, it didn't take long to come to an agreement.

With a picture book as a guide, Antonio taught himself how to remove and replace the rusted tin and to bring the finish of the wood back to life. It had been careful but therapeutic work, especially as he actually intended to use the refurbished piece. He had since kept the trunk in the bedroom where he stored seasonal clothes in the bottom, and in the liftout tray beneath the lid, he kept the few things he had brought with him in his escape from America.

"Why do you call it an 'escape'?" a neighbor had once asked. "Why would you escape?"

Antonio wasn't sure how to respond but knew he needed a positive description, a way that would make his leaving America inevitable.

"Too many women," he had said in his nascent Italian, to which the neighbor responded with a laugh and a phrase that took Antonio a moment to translate.

"Too many women? Or too many husbands?"

Antonio opened the trunk. In the liftout tray, he had a custom-made pair of Charlie Dunn western boots and a faded drugstore envelope with photos.

Antonio no longer wore the boots. When he'd had the heels repaired by a local Italian shoemaker two years after his arrival, they lost their familiar fit. With more symbolism than practicality, Antonio had polished them one last time and put them away.

The photos were from a party. A beer and pizza blowout near a lake in Austin, Texas, where the host was named Bubba, and where Antonio took Brenda Anne Beinecke on their first outing together.

Mixed in with the photos was a smaller envelope, in it the letter that had helped to push him into exile. The letter was a note from the same Miss Beinecke, neatly written on folded thirty-two pound stationery. He had memorized the lines the first and only time he read it before slipping it back into its envelope never to answer.

Antonio started to remove the liftout tray but instead sat on the floor next to his bed with a thud. He felt heavy. It had happened before: a morning sadness before his first cappuccino that he could not push away. And as he had done with increasing frequency, Antonio covered his eyes with his hand and started to cry.

☐   ☐   ☐

My Dearest Eddie,

This last month has been the happiest of my life. You have touched me in ways I could never imagine. You have taught me things about myself I had never known. You have shown me how to love in a way I thought only existed on the pages of books or between the lines of poems. You have helped me realize the only thing I want is to spend the rest of my life with you.

Yours only and forever,
Brenda Anne

☐   ☐   ☐

By the time Antonio bicycled over the bridge into the neighboring town, word had spread about the latest collapse. When he entered the building where he worked, several on the ground floor asked if he'd been affected. "*Solo un po,*" he answered. Only a little.

He shouldered his bike up two flights to his office.

"Ah, *buongiorno*, Antonio," Josephina greeted him.

"*Buongiorno*," he answered, his Italian still heavy with the American accent that his coworkers had come to forgive.

"Sorry to hear about the collapse," she said in Italian.

He waved it away. "It's nothing," he said. "Living where I do is not for men afraid of sailing off the edge of the earth."

He leaned his bicycle on the wall next to his desk, then opened the window. The air conditioning was spotty. The owner of the business would walk through the rooms after everyone left each day making sure all units were off and all lights were out. In the morning, it took a while for the temperature to drop to a comfortable level. Antonio leaned on the sill and looked down the street. It was an old building with walls of thick stone. Antonio liked the solidness of it. The street was narrow, with barely room for two cars to pass. The buildings were centuries old, and the grooved cobblestones and worn alley steps testament to its history.

The streets and passages didn't look that different from those Antonio saw from the front window of his house. The secret of his street was the fickleness of the earth below it.

Ten minutes earlier, he had stopped at the corner café and shot back a cappuccino. It would be his breakfast. He sat at his desk. As he reached for the keyboard to boot up his computer, his hands shook. His fingers twitched and fought him as he tried to type in his password. He clasped his hands, squeezing the fingers between one another, but when he pulled them apart, the shaking had not lessened. He flattened his palms on the surface of his desk, forcing them to be still. Five seconds, ten seconds. When he lifted them, the tremors had decreased. He entered his password.

"Everything okay?"

Antonio looked up. Josephina stood in the doorway.

"Yes, why?"

She shifted her weight. "I saw your hands. And your face is pale."

She stepped inside and closed the door behind her. "It's the anniversary, isn't it? Adelina's accident."

He and Josephina had often flirted before Adelina died. Since, she had softened her playful ambiguity. It puzzled him until he realized it was simply that she no longer saw him as a safe married man, someone out of reach, someone with whom she could play suggestively without the messy follow through.

"I'm sorry," she said.

He shook his head, "It's okay." He gave her the story of Adelina's ashes mixed with the dirt of her garden dissipating in that morning's breeze.

She came around the desk and knelt by the arm of his chair. She touched his face, then pulled her hand away, holding it against her chest. "Real love doesn't come that often," she said. "I understand."

He looked at her, struck by the simple thought. He nodded, then surprised them both by starting to cry. Josephina leaned over and held him. He cried on her shoulder. When he pulled away, he had no words to tell her that what he was grieving was not the unlucky Adelina, struck down before her time, but the foolish loss of a young American girl from whom he had run away decades earlier. And for the first time, he wondered if his hidden fantasy of finding her again might really be possible. Or safe.

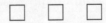

On this day thirty years before, Antonio Enzo Marino, known to his Austin friends as Eddie Enzo, had been a happy guy. Young, single, and less than a semester short of finishing his MFA at the flagship campus of the University of Texas, he had spent the early morning hours with Michelle, tapping on her bedroom window well after midnight. They had an agreement, he and Michelle. Either could call the other with no strings. She would unlock the slider, and he could slip into her bedroom without waking her kids. She'd pull him into her under the covers, and afterward, share a silent cigarette. Sometimes she'd hold him for a while but never complained if he left the bed without ever turning on the light. Only once had she questioned him, frustrated that she hadn't been able to find him one night when her ex had the kids. "I really wanted you," she had said, then apologized before he could even respond.

Michelle knew that he visited at least two others. And each of those suspected the same with different degrees of forgiveness. It was complicated, especially as one of the ladies happened to share his two-bedroom apartment.

On that day, almost noon, he sat by the pool, soaking in the sun. When he had gotten home just before dawn, he'd found his apartment mate, Alice, asleep in his room. He was going to take a shower but didn't want to raise suspicion. When Alice stirred, he feared she would wake to the smell of his detour, so he worked below the sheets to arouse and confuse her senses. Afterward, she slipped back into sleep, and midmorning he escaped to the pool to be cleansed by the chlorine.

Alice worked multiple shifts at an all-night diner and was supposed to work that afternoon. Eddie would wait until she was safely out of the apartment before phoning Chloe.

Chloe. The married one. The most dangerous of the three. Chloe. Married to a cop.

"He's harmless," she'd said to Eddie the first time she mentioned her husband. "We haven't lived together in months. And what I do is none of his goddamn business."

Eddie had met Chloe at a downtown Austin bar. She was with a couple of girl pals smoking, drinking, and watching Longhorns basketball. He'd bummed a light and a cigarette, then entertained her with made-up stories about the players. She knew he was blowing smoke but played along. When he walked her to her car, she rolled down the window.

"I sure enjoyed funning with you this evening," she had said, and before she could add anything, Eddie leaned through the window and kissed her.

"Oh my," was her response. "Maybe the evening ain't over."

He had followed her home, ignoring the headlights behind him.

She didn't confess to having an estranged husband until the second time he'd spent the night. Only then did Eddie remember that when he had left her apartment that first morning, a car had followed him back to his building.

The next week, as he was about to leave his apartment one night, he saw a patrol car cruising the lot. It glided past his door, spotlight checking license tags on the cars parked across from him. Eddie hid inside, watching. The car wasn't a local. The graphics on the side identified a jurisdiction several miles north. Risky, Eddie thought. Man on duty crossing the line.

"That was probably Ivan," Chloe said. "He's spooked a couple a my boyfriends just cruising around. Just letting me and them know he's there." They were lying on her sofa where Chloe had dared him to meet during her lunch hour. He'd rushed to her apartment from campus, parking on the far side of her building. He walked quickly, checking behind him, and ducked inside as soon as she opened the door. They never made it to the bedroom. Afterward, still breathing hard, Eddie told her about the morning patrol.

She held out two fingers for a cigarette. He pulled one out of a pack and wedged it into the V. She waited for him to light it. "He'll never do anything," she said. "Underneath all that macho cop bullshit, he's afraid a me."

Chloe blew smoke toward the ceiling, then reached for her clothes. "Baby, I gotta go. You want to hang for a bit, that's okay. Just lock the door when you leave."

"How can you be so sure?" asked Eddie. "That he'd never do anything."

"I was with him a long time," she said. "I gave him a lot to be pissed about. Nothing ever happened."

Eddie pulled on his jeans. "But if something did happen, I don't want to be the one it happens to."

Chloe pushed him back onto the couch and straddled his lap. "Let me tell you something about Ivan," she said, reaching over him to stub out the cigarette in the end table ashtray. "One time we'd been drinkin' with one a his buddies, Gene Dixon. We'd all had a little too much. Gene says we should go for a ride, clear our heads. Ivan drives radio blastin'. Me and Gene in the back, riding each other like a couple a high school kids. I know Ivan could hear us. I think he even turned around a couple a times. But he just cranked up the music and kept on driving. When we sat up, I climbed into the front. Ivan didn't say shit. Just headed home while I buttoned my blouse. Ivan gets outta the car, unlocks the front door, and Gene gives me one last feel. Ivan sees him, turns around, and goes inside."

"Jesus," said Eddie. "He's getting his gun."

"He's getting nothing. He calls me in, we get undressed, he goes to bed, and falls asleep while I'm rinsin' Gene outta my panties."

Chloe got off of him and finished getting dressed. "If he didn't kill me 'n' Gene right then and there, he ain't gonna do shit." She shook out her hair and grabbed her purse. "I gotta get back to work. If I'm late again, I'll have to go in on Saturday." She leaned forward as if to kiss him but licked his cheek instead. "See you tonight?"

"Maybe," said Eddie.

"Half a lunch hour's not long enough to do it right," she said with a smile, then disappeared out the door.

A couple of minutes later, Eddie was ready to leave. He looked out the window. The patrol car was there, right across from the door. And so was Ivan, leaning back against the fender. His uniform was sharp, regulation creases on his shirt, badge shiny, reflector sunglasses masking his eyes. His arms were crossed. He was waiting.

A neighbor came out of her door. "Hi, Ivan," she said with a wave. "Haven't seen you in a while. Everything okay?" She was barefoot, wearing jeans and a t-shirt, holding a book as if she'd been reading. Eddie had seen her before. Chloe said she and her roommate were students at the university.

Ivan nodded, "Been better," he said.

"Sorry to hear about you and Chloe," she said.

He nodded again. "Shit happens."

"You on duty?" she asked. "Want to come in for a minute? Have something cold?"

"No, thanks," he said. "I just came by to check on the place. Still paying the rent." He turned and opened the driver's door.

"Sure, okay," the neighbor said with a smile. "It's good to see you. Always felt safer with you next door."

He got in the car and slowly drove away. The neighbor stood in the drive watching him leave, then turned to Eddie at the window. She smiled and gave a little wave. He opened the door. "Hi," she said. "I'm Brenda Anne. I live next door."

"Yeah," he said. "I've seen you."

"I lied when I told him I always felt safer with him around," she said. "Truth is, he scares the hell out of me."

"Chloe says he's harmless."

"I don't think so," she said. "I think he's a tickin' bomb ready to go off. Maybe this isn't the safest place for you to be."

Sometimes when he'd had too much wine, like the evening following the loss of Adelina's garden, Antonio would take out the envelope from his trunk and look through the pictures. There were people whose names he could no longer remember. Fellow students at the university with whom he had spent long hours in the design studios and with whom he had traveled to the most god-awful bars in a half-hour radius of Austin.

Brenda Anne would be in her fifties now. The last time he held the photo, he tried to imagine how she might look, but he couldn't. He couldn't imagine anything except how she smiled when he touched her.

Antonio closed the trunk and sat next to his bed for a long moment. He wondered if she had ever tried to find him.

"Antonio!" he imagined her calling his name. "Antonio." But she never knew him by Antonio. Only by Eddie. And with a different last name.

He was only six when he and his mother fled her abusive marriage in the middle of a starless night. They traveled two days by bus and started over in a Texas town north of Austin. His mom got a job in a restaurant and managed to enroll him in school using his father's first name and his own middle one. Since then, everyone only knew him as Eddie Enzo.

If Brenda Anne Beinecke had ever tried to find him, it would be a quick dead end. There was no way she'd be able to uncover the family name he'd reclaimed.

That lunch hour when Brenda Anne rescued him from Ivan the Cop had been the start. She had invited him in for a minute in case Ivan came back for one more circle of the building. She offered him a Coke and lunch. He surprised himself when he said yes.

"I like Chloe," she said. "She's been a good neighbor to me and my roommate."

"I like her, too," said Eddie.

Brenda Anne laughed. "I can tell. The walls ain't that thick."

Eddie felt himself redden. "Sorry," he said, suppressing a smile.

"That's okay," said Brenda Anne. "It's nice hearing you and Chloe express yourselves."

It was her openness and lack of pretense that had appealed to him. She asked about his program at the university and seemed flattered when he asked about hers.

"Psychology," she answered. "With a minor in lit. I guess I'm just one a them romantic college girls trying to figure herself out."

"What's to figure out?"

"Oh, you know," she said. "Why we are the way we are."

"And how would you describe yourself?"

She looked at him across the table. He knew she was wondering if he wanted a real answer or not.

"Seriously," he added to make it clear.

"Shy. Quiet. Curious."

"Curious about what?"

"Curious about lots of things."

"Give me one example."

She smiled, radiant. "You."

It was easier for Antonio to find her than he expected. He started with a simple online search using her full name. There were no exact matches. Social media searches were no more fertile.

The alumni site for the university showed that she had graduated and gave a married name. It took a half hour to discover that she had divorced and remarried and another hour to identify a double handful of possibilities. Those he narrowed to a pool of half a dozen.

He sought for pictures. There were dozens, almost all false combinations of names or references, except for three. One was a woman about the right age, speaking at a local fundraising event outside of Chicago. Another was a twenty-something who had a vague resemblance to his memory of Brenda Anne. And the third was a copy of the same photo Antonio had kept secreted in his trunk for all of these years.

Two evenings after Brenda Anne had expressed her curiosity about Eddie Enzo, he was in the middle of another dangerous liaison with Chloe. They were on her bed, headboard knocking against the wall, and Eddie aware that Brenda Anne was just a few feet away on the other side. Earlier in the evening, the thought excited him. But in the reality of the moment, he lost his passion and dropped helplessly next to Chloe, leaving her puzzled and frustrated. She was not sympathetic, and when she raised her voice, Eddie pulled on his jeans and left.

He drove across town to Michelle's and knocked on her bedroom window. She unlocked the slider but surprised him when she opened it only a crack and told him it wasn't a good time. When he pressed, she confessed that her ex was spending the night.

He drove to his apartment. Alice was working the overnight at the restaurant. He took a shower, then called Brenda Anne.

It had been a quiet conversation. He told her he had been at Chloe's earlier in the evening.

"I know," Brenda Anne said.

"Sorry about that," he said.

"I have to admit, I was glad when I heard you leave."

They were on the phone almost an hour when Brenda Anne told him her roommate wouldn't be home that evening. It took Eddie another ten minutes before he asked if he could come by.

"Do you think that would be safe?" she asked. "I mean, what if Chloe found out."

"She won't find out," he said.

After a long pause, Brenda Anne said, "Okay," then hung up.

Eddie parked in the lot the farthest from her building, then sneaked to Brenda Anne's door. It opened before he could knock.

"Hi," she said.

"Hi."

"I'm glad you called. Want a beer?"

They sat on the couch and talked in hushed tones, aware that danger lurked just yards away.

"You know," said Brenda Anne. "You're not the only one who visits her."

It caught him by surprise. He hadn't really thought about Chloe entertaining others.

"But we can tell she likes you the best."

Eddie must have looked puzzled.

"My roommate and me. We listen sometimes."

Eddie reddened. "So why do you say she likes me the best?"

Brenda Anne just smiled.

That first visit, they spent a chaste night wrapped around each other on Brenda Anne's couch. In the morning, Brenda Anne watched for Chloe to leave before Eddie slipped away.

The next day, Eddie met Brenda Anne on campus. She sat barefoot with him on the grass outside the student union. She laughed at his jokes and pulled him into an honest discussion about the seventeenth century English poet, John Donne.

"Jack Donne in his early years," she said. "Beautiful, sexual poems hidden under layers of metaphor."

"How do you know so much about this?"

"I'd better know it," she said. "I have an exam tomorrow."

Eddie had never liked poetry. But when Brenda Anne read him lines from Donne's "To His Mistress Going to Bed," he became a believer. He asked if she would like to slip away and mimic Donne's observations.

"I think," she said with a smile, "I'm not quite ready to jeopardize our newfound friendship."

The next day they spent an hour on the phone talking about art and design. That evening, in hushed voices on her couch, they

shared childhood stories and future hopes, and sometime near midnight also shared the vulnerability that comes with being new lovers.

Eddie was surprised that he was her first.

"I trust you," she said.

The next night, Eddie visited Michelle.

Antonio told his boss he was going on holiday and closed up the
house.

"I will miss you," said Josephina, who had volunteered to drive
him to the Rome airport. "I wish I was going with you."

"I think your husband would object," he said.

She laughed. "If he noticed I was gone."

Josephina grew up in Rome and drove like it. She wove the Fiat
fearlessly through traffic, never signaling, never using the rearview
mirror.

"I am a little jealous," she said. "I know you're meeting a woman."

"You always think I'm meeting a woman."

"But this time I know it."

"And how is that?"

"I can smell it," she said.

Antonio shifted in the seat. "I think your nose deceives you."

She looked at him, longer than was comfortable.

Antonio liked Josephina's intensity. She was always the first one
in a meeting to object if something seemed wrong.

"*Stupido!*" she would spit out. And most often she was right.

Antonio liked to watch her when she was angry and often wondered what she would be like as a lover. Even now there were those
moments when he knew she wondered the same about him.

At the terminal, she stood next to the car, arms crossed as he pulled his pack from the back.

"You're not coming back, are you," she said, anger in her voice usually reserved for their boss.

"I'm coming back," he said, slinging the pack over his shoulder.

"If you leave me here alone, *sel un imbicile*, I will hunt you and kill you and eat you."

"I'm coming back," he repeated as she grabbed both his cheeks and gave him a hard kiss.

When he tried to embrace her, she shoved him away, got back in the car, slammed the door, and raced off without a backward glance. He stood on the curb until the Fiat disappeared in the traffic, then turned and walked into the terminal.

During the years he had lived in Italy, Antonio kept his US passport current. Traveling in Europe was easier with his Italian passport, but using it to enter the United States would limit his stay. And what he would not confess to Josephina was that he did not know how long he would stay.

It was a direct flight into New York—almost seven hours—but with the time change it was still late afternoon when he arrived.

Antonio had not tried to contact Brenda Anne. He was afraid how she might react, how easy it would be for her to be furious. Or worse, report the contact to police. In Texas, as in most states, there was no statute of limitation for the crime he had committed.

Eddie Enzo was confused. He had been seeing Brenda Anne for almost a month. He was still juggling visits with Michelle and long evenings in between with his apartment mate, Alice. But there was something different about his time with Brenda Anne. There was an honesty and openness to her he had not experienced with anyone before. They had met away from her apartment several times during that month. She had even spent an evening at his place when Alice had pulled an all-nighter at the restaurant. But he was nervous that they might be discovered, and he was relieved when Brenda Anne left before midnight.

One night after music, beer, and nachos, Eddie found them a motel room off the interstate, south of the city. "We won't have to worry about who might be listening," he said. And despite the surf of traffic from the nearby highway, thumping music from the bar below, and unknown voices on the other side of the wall, it was one of the best times they had together.

"I think I love you, Eddie Enzo," Brenda Anne had said as he was falling asleep. He didn't know what to say and just wrapped an arm around her. In a few minutes, she was asleep. He was wide awake.

Two days later coming out of class, he found her note tucked under a wiper on his windshield. He got behind the wheel and opened it. He read it once, then sat for almost a half hour before folding it back into its envelope.

During that month he had not visited Chloe, which was not to say he hadn't thought of it. But the logistics were beyond him. If he sneaked into her apartment, he knew Brenda Anne would hear all but the quietest conversations. He did call Chloe. Twice. The second time, she called him back.

"You're an asshole," she said when he answered the phone. "First you don't finish what you start, then you just walk out? No explanation? And you don't even have the balls to call me for a month? What kind a chickenshit is that?"

"I'm sorry," was all he could muster.

She was silent for a moment, then said, "Apology accepted. But you're still an asshole."

"How you doing?"

"Randy," she said. "Wouldn't mind if you came over and humped it outta me."

Eddie switched the phone to his other ear. "That would be nice," he said, "but I can't tonight."

"Visiting one of your other little friends?"

"No."

"You think I don't know about them?"

Eddie stopped breathing.

"Don't get your panties in a bunch," she said. "We never took an oath. You have your friends, I have mine. It's okay."

"It's not that."

"What then? Your roommate home?"

"No."

"Then come on over. Have a beer. I'll let you loose before she gets off work."

"I never told you about my roommate."

"I'm not just a pretty face with a hot body," she said. "I know more than you think I do."

Eddie sat on his couch.

"You still there?" Chloe asked.

"Yeah."

"Don't think about it. Just come."

Eddie parked in a distant corner of the lot. It was dark, and he hid behind the cars across from the front of Chloe's building. Brenda Anne's lights were off so he made a brisk crossing to Chloe's door. She opened it on the first knock.

"You may be an asshole," she said, locking the door behind him, "but I kinda missed you."

In less than a minute, she had pulled him into the bedroom.

"That was fun," she said afterward.

"Nice to know you missed me," Eddie said.

They lay in the dark for a while. Eddie thought Chloe had fallen asleep.

"I know about Brenda Anne, too," she said.

Eddie wasn't sure how to respond. "How?" he finally asked.

"Ivan. He was following you for a while. Couldn't wait to tell me about it."

"Wow," said Eddie. "You okay?"

Chloe reached over and patted his cheek. "I'm fine," she said. "Made him a little crazy, though."

"Crazy crazy?"

"Just a tad. Said he was going to kill you."

□   □   □

Antonio was bewildered by the changes in the town he had left behind. It started when he landed at the airport, a metropolis southeast of the one he remembered.

He got lost twice trying to find his old apartment. It took a while for him to realize it had long been swallowed by the ever-expanding university.

Antonio knew where Brenda Anne Jordan lived. He knew where she worked. He knew she had two grown children from her first marriage. He knew that she had been married this time for a dozen years. And after making an anonymous call to her office, he knew she was not at work that day.

He parked across the street from her house, an upscale contemporary in a development near Lake Austin. It was not an inexpensive home. There was an expensive import in the driveway.

Antonio Enzo Marino—Eddie Enzo—got out of his car. He took a breath, and before he could change his mind, walked up the drive and rang the bell.

It took a moment for the door to open.

Brenda Anne Beinecke had barely aged a day since he had last seen her.

"Brenda Anne," he said.

"Yes?" she said.

"Brenda Anne, it's me, Eddie."

"Oh," she smiled. "I think you want Brenda Anne the mother, not Brenda Anne the daughter. I'll get her."

Before he could respond, she left him standing on the stoop.

"Yes?"

This Brenda Anne was thirty years older than the surrogate. She was taller than he remembered, almost his height. Thinner, too. If he had passed her on the street, he wouldn't have recognized her. Her hair was tied back, lighter than the photo. She was tan with damage from the dry Texas sun. Her neck was thin, and her eyes darker than the bright blue he'd remembered. Her face was creased. He wondered if he looked as timeworn to her as she did to him. She had been working in the yard—V-neck t-shirt, shorts, and barefoot. She was holding a pair of garden gloves.

"Hi," he said. "It's me. Eddie. Enzo."

"I know who you are," she said and looked at him for a long minute before moving back to let him in.

He stepped forward to hug her. She put up her hand. They sat across from each other in the front room. It was large and open with contemporary art adorning the walls and a mix of sculptures breaking up the space. Eddie tried to imagine her entertaining here, mingling with guests, laughing at their jokes, standing tall, barefoot, and wearing something he would have never seen her in. She sat back in the chair, legs crossed, the only sign of discomfort a bobbing foot, revealing a black bottom.

"Why are you here?" she asked, voice polite but firm.

"I don't know how to start," he said.

"Why don't you start by telling me what you're doing here? In my house. Thirty years after you ran away."

"I wanted to see you. I wanted to tell you that I'm sorry."

"Sorry for what, exactly?"

"Sorry for everything."

She almost laughed. "Eddie Enzo, you're a piece of work. Thirty years late and that's the best line you got?"

"I'm sorry for leaving."

"Leaving without a word."

"I couldn't risk it."

"You couldn't risk a call from some payphone? Or a note? Something to let me know you were alive?"

"I couldn't take the chance."

"And now you show up at my door a lifetime later."

She sat, arms crossed, looking at him.

"I was afraid they might have your phone tapped or be checking your mail. It was one of their own that got shot."

"He was a crazy bastard," said Brenda Anne. "They knew that. He killed his wife and shot himself."

"He didn't shoot himself," said Eddie. "He caught us together.

Shot her point blank, then came after me. We fought in the kitch-en. The gun went off."

"And then you ran."

"Yes. I ran," said Eddie. "Because I knew you heard it all."

"Momma?" Brenda Anne's daughter interrupted from the kitchen. "You want me to fix some iced tea for you and Mr. Enzo?"

"No thank you, dear," she answered. "He'll be leaving soon."

Brenda Anne, hands now in her lap, nodded. "Yes, I knew you were there with her," she said. "That was the hardest thing to get past. That you were so self-centered and so blatant in your disre-gard for me, that you'd be with her on the other side of that wall."

Eddie took a breath.

"Don't," said Brenda Anne. "Don't you dare say you're sorry."

"But," he started to say before she raised her hand to silence him.

"I was the only one who knew you were there," said Brenda Anne. "And despite it all, I never told them a thing. They closed it as a 'murder suicide.' You didn't have to run. You didn't have to leave. And it would have been easy for you to find out and come back. But you didn't."

"I'm not that Eddie Enzo anymore," he said. "I'm not that guy. And I've regretted leaving, leaving you, almost every day."

This time Brenda Anne did laugh. "Oh, Jesus," she said. "Do you have any idea how pathetic that sounds?" She shook her head. "Have you noticed I haven't asked you where you were all this time, Eddie Enzo? It's because I. Don't. Care. And I haven't cared for twenty-nine of those thirty years. Yes, when you first left I was devastated. And I waited for you. But when I didn't hear from you, I realized that you had gone and done me the biggest favor. When I thought of what you were like, how little you loved or respected me, your leaving set me free. So, no pitiful apologies necessary," she said as she stood and crossed to the door. "Instead, let me thank you, Eddie Enzo." She pulled the door open. "Thank you for saving me from the black misery of any failed time we would have had together. My life didn't end when you left. It began."

"You came back," Josephina said when she picked up Antonio at the airport. "I didn't think you would."

"How could I ever leave you?" Antonio smiled.

"My husband thinks we are lovers," she said as she maneuvered them into the traffic.

"And what did you tell him?"

"That if we were lovers he would never know."

Antonio laughed.

Josephina shot them across two lanes with barely a glance behind her.

"I do have some bad news," she said. "Your yard is smaller than when you left. There was another tremor."

"How much smaller?"

"Maybe half a meter," she said.

Antonio took a deep breath. "That's a lot. Maybe it's time for me to move," he said.

"And why would you move?" asked Josephina. "You have no use for a yard."

Josephina lowered her window to curse a driver who had tried to cut them off. When she turned to Antonio to complain about the idiots they let use Italian roads, he answered her with a broad smile.

She was quiet when they made their way onto the long high-way out of the city.

"May I ask you something?" she said.

"Of course."

"Did you find the woman?"

"Yes," he said.

"I knew it!" she chastised. "I knew it was a woman."

Antonio only nodded.

"And was she as you had remembered?"

"Her feet were dirty," he said.

Josephina looked at him.

They were quiet for several minutes.

"If we were lovers," she said as if there had been no break in the conversation, "do you know where we would make love tonight?"

"In my yard?"

"Yes!" she laughed. "Close to the edge. We would tempt fate."

She dropped him in the parking lot near the bridge that he would walk up to his village.

"I am glad you came back," she said, kissing him on both cheeks.

"Thank you for coming to get me."

"*Ciao*, Antonio," she said and sped away.

Antonio was exhausted by the time he opened his front door. It had been a long day, and the sun was slipping away. He dropped his pack and poured a glass of wine. He sat on the back stoop and looked at his shrinking yard, wondering how much longer he might have left. He finished the glass and went into the bedroom. He opened the trunk and took out Brenda Anne's photo and letter. In the fading light, he crawled across his yard and sat cross-legged near the edge. He slid the photo into the envelope with the note, then ripped them both into small pieces. As the shadow of darkness spread across his yard, Antonio threw the confetti toward the edge. The evening breeze caught it and swept it over the valley.

DOIN' THE LAUNDRY

Ron-Allen Tucker knew his wife had decided to kill him. It was a Saturday morning at 10:18. She was doing the laundry. He came in from the garage and saw her standing in front of the washing machine, back toward him, detergent cup in hand. The old dryer was thumping loudly, otherwise she would have heard him. She hesitated, then poured in the liquid. All of it. A full cup. A new detergent with stain fighters and a fragrance to which she knew he was allergic.

He banged the door. She spun around.

"Hi," he said.

"I'm doin' the laundry," she said.

"Great."

"It was dirty."

"I hope so."

She scowled and turned back to the washer, closing the lid.

There was a time when Patti would have laughed. A dozen years ago, when they first started dating after high school, she enjoyed his sense of humor. It was different from hers. "Unexpected," was how she had described it. "You see things so differently than I do," she had told him. "It makes me smile."

And for a long time, she smiled and laughed at his silly jokes and observations, often repeating them to her sister Elise, who now lived across the street.

But she hadn't been smiling lately. Maybe six months. Maybe a year. Maybe two.

The time had sneaked up on him. He wasn't sure how long her feelings toward him had been waning before he'd noticed. It was a gradual thing. He'd chuckle at something on the tube. She'd change the channel.

"I was watching that," he'd complain.

"It's dumb," she'd say, then skip through a dozen shows until she landed on some program in which he had no interest.

Or he'd cut out a cartoon from the newspaper and put it on the refrigerator. In the beginning, she'd shake her head and laugh, but over the last months, she ignored them.

"Did you see the new one?" he'd ask.

"I saw it," was all she would say.

He stopped cutting them out.

Their lovemaking was another thing—slow, subtle shifts that fooled him into thinking he was getting bored. She'd never been comfortable talking about sex. Especially early on. He could embarrass her with a leer or an unexpected grope. She'd redden but would often lead him into the bedroom. If she had a beer or two, she'd let herself enjoy the attention he'd pay to her body and welcome his excitement. Afterward in the dark, if he asked how it was, she'd confess, "Ron-Allen, you take me places I like to visit," then bury her face in his side.

They slipped from four or five encounters a week, to two or three. Then one. Now they skipped whole weeks entirely. Patti's confessions of passion morphed into declarations of fatigue. Or headache. For a while he did worry about her health. Even suggested she see her doctor. She took his concern as criticism and met it with anger. Occasionally, when apathy gave in to appetite, her frenzied movements were automatic. And while he believed no orgasm was a bad orgasm, Patti seemed to take little pleasure in the release. When they'd finish, she would turn her back to him and lie distant, feigning sleep.

The phone rang. A second time. Ron-Allen picked it up, but Patti had gotten to it first.

"Patti." It was Elise. "This afternoon?"

Ron-Allen was about to hang up but hesitated when he heard his wife answer in a whisper. "He's been workin' in the garage. I'll call you as soon as he leaves."

Ron-Allen had barely gotten the phone on the hook when Patti walked in.

"If you're goin' out," she said, "we need milk."

"I wasn't planning on it," he said. "I'm in the middle of tuning my truck. Going up to the lake tomorrow."

"Well, take mine. We need milk. If you don't get it now, there won't be any in the mornin'."

He opened the refrigerator. There was a gallon jug almost a third full.

"That's spoiled," she said and grabbed it, dumping it down the sink. "And pick me up a pack a smokes."

"I thought you were trying to quit," he said.

She ignored him again and put the empty jug into the trash.

Patti drove a big SUV. "I want to sit up high," she'd said. "I'm tired of lookin' at the ass end of all them soccer-mom minivans."

Ron-Allen backed out of the driveway and headed up their suburban street. He turned the corner, then doubled back and parked near the end of the block.

Just as he thought, Elise and her preteen daughter, Alison, were making a beeline directly toward his house. The front door opened before they got to it and closed quickly behind them.

Ron-Allen climbed down from the seat.

"Need some help?" a voice asked. Ron-Allen's neighbor, Fred Gavus, was watering his lawn. "Truck okay?"

"Yeah," Ron-Allen waved. "Forgot something. Need the exercise. Patti's taking a nap. Don't wanna wake her." His responses sounded lame, especially since Fred had probably seen Elise and Alison charging into the house.

"Well," Fred chuckled. "Don't git yourself shot sneaking in the back."

Ron-Allen looked over at him, but Fred had already turned away to hose the dying shrub under his living room window.

The front yards on the street were all open. The backs were all fenced—and not subtly. People liked their privacy here. The fences were tall and tight, blocking any casual view from a neighbor. Ron-Allen cut across his driveway and into the open garage. He cracked the backdoor a notch and surveyed his backyard. Above-ground pool, neatly trimmed grass. Gas grill on the deck. No sign of Patti or Elise. He slipped into the yard and ducked behind the rhododendrons. The girls would most likely be in the kitchen. He eased his way beneath the window. It was open.

"Whatcha doin', Daddy?"

The voice startled him. Eight-year-old Bobbi had popped out from behind the deck. She stood looking at him, smiling, knowing she had caught him doing something he probably shouldn't be.

"I'm checking the bushes," he said. "See if they got bugs or need feedin'."

"Momma says she's gonna cut 'em down first chance she gets." Bobbi moved closer to him under the open window.

"Momma didn't exactly mean that," Ron-Allen said.

"Momma didn't exactly mean what?" Patti asked above them.

"Momma, Daddy says he's gonna feed the ugly bushes," Bobbi said, yanking at the leaves.

Patti lifted the screen and leaned out the window. "Ron-Allen, what are you doin' back here? You're supposed to be at the store. And where's my truck?"

Bobbi plopped herself on the grass to watch.

"I'm checking the bushes for bugs. Gonna get some poison while I'm at the store."

It was a weak response.

"You've got poison in the garage," Patti said. "Three cans and two bottles."

"Different poison for different bugs," he said.

It was a reasonable response. Patti hesitated.

"Where's my truck?" she asked again.

"Up the block. I didn't want you heckling me about forgettin' somethin'."

A brilliant response. How could she argue against that?

She glared at him, then slammed the screen and the window. He turned around. Bobbi was already across the yard, kicking at a ball, probably disappointed that the crisis had such a simple and quiet resolution.

Ron-Allen was pleased with himself and headed back up the street. It was only after he got behind the wheel that he realized his reconnaissance had utterly failed. And that Patti knew exactly how much poison he had on the top shelf in the garage.

"Shoot."

Ron-Allen hurried to the store. He picked up a gallon of milk, two packs of Patti's menthols, and a can of the mildest bug spray he could find. *Safe to use with pets and kids!*

The house was empty when he returned. No sign of Patti or Bobbi or Elise or Alison. Patti couldn't have gone too far; he had her truck. Maybe she was across the street plotting with her sister. He opened the refrigerator to put away the milk. There were two sirloins marinating in separate dishes. He closed the door, then immediately reopened it. Separate dishes when each was big enough for both pieces of meat.

He heard someone come in the front. He switched the dishes just as his wife entered the room.

"Your cigarettes are on the table," he said.

"Damn it, Ron-Allen. I said one pack not two. You know I'm tryin' to cut down. You tryin' to kill me?"

"You're welcome," he said and headed into the garage.

He checked the poisons on his shelf. Three cans and two bottles, just as Patti had said. One of the bottles was almost empty. He took a felt-tip pen from his workbench and marked the levels on each container.

That evening at dinner, Patti seemed to be in a good mood. Bobbi was having a sleepover at Alison's. The TV was on, but the sound was turned down. The house was quiet.

"Ron-Allen, you're just pickin' at your steak."

"I'm not too hungry."

"Elise found the recipe for the marinade. It's good, don't you think?"

"Tasty."

Patti took the last forkful from her plate and smiled as she slipped it into her mouth. He watched as she chewed and swallowed.

"I made my special dessert," she said.

"Strawberry cheesecake?"

"Um hmm."

She cleared the dishes from the table and brought them each a piece. When she went back to the kitchen for the topping, he switched the plates.

She spooned out whipped cream. He was surprised when she took a dollop on her finger and licked it off.

"Want to have dessert upstairs?" she asked.

He followed her to their bedroom. She closed the door, pulled the shade, and led him to the bed. For the first time in months, she kissed him. It was a passionate kiss—something he'd almost forgotten. He was surprised at how quickly he ignored all suspicion. He took a deep breath and put his hand on her waist, reaching under her blouse. He felt her tremble, then shudder. And just as he was about to touch her breast, he felt her stomach rumble, a resonant growl that heaved her dinner all over the bed.

She sat up, clutching her belly and threw up again, this time catching him point blank.

"You okay?" he asked as she stumbled into the bathroom.

She slammed the door behind her. He heard her upchuck again, flushing the toilet several times. He took off his soiled clothes, stripped the bed, and carted everything down to the laundry room. By the time he got back, Patti was lying on the bedroom floor.

"You okay?" he asked again.

She opened one eye and glared at him. "Oh yeah," she said. "Never better." She rolled onto her side and pulled a throw rug over her.

Ron-Allen took a shower, then made up the bed. By the time he crawled between the clean sheets, Patti was snoring.

He slept fitfully. Twice he woke with a start, thinking his wife was standing above him. Each time, he looked apprehensively over the edge of the bed to assure himself that Patti was still asleep on the floor. He tossed and turned until he saw dawn around the edge of the window shade. He gave up, got up, and headed for the kitchen to put on a pot of coffee.

He had left the laundry room door open. The smell of the soiled bed clothes permeated the air. He stuffed them in the washer. He found his detergent hidden behind the bleach, poured in a cup, and started the machine. Back in the kitchen, he noticed another pungent smell. He traced it to the open container of dessert topping Patti had left on the dining room table. He dumped it in the sink and washed it away, noting that the sell-by date was weeks in the past.

While the coffee brewed, he fixed a bowl of cereal. He tried to read the paper but couldn't concentrate. By the time he was done eating, Patti had made her way into the kitchen.

"Good morning," he said. He almost asked her how she was feeling but didn't feel like starting the day with a glare. He got one anyway.

Patti poured a cup of coffee and sat across from him. She took the first section of the paper and hid behind it while he put his cup in the sink.

"You still drivin' up to the lake this mornin'?" she asked.

"Yeah," he answered. "Want to try that new rod."

"What time you plannin' on being home?"

"Usual," he said.

"What time?"

"Three. Maybe four."

He went upstairs and got dressed. When he returned to the kitchen, Patti was still buried in the paper but had packed him a lunch—a sandwich, an apple, and a snack bag of corn chips.

He gave her a kiss on the cheek. "Have a good day, sweetie."

"I plan to," she said and turned the page.

The lake was an hour away. He liked heading up there whenever he got a chance. The drive relaxed him. Patti and Bobbi used to come, but his wife didn't like the sun, and his daughter was always bored. They'd both complain, and he'd have to leave hours before he was ready. The truth was he enjoyed the time away from the Tucker women. And it made it easier to keep his secret—that he didn't really care much for fishing. What he did enjoy was parking his truck under a tree near the shore, sitting in a folding chair facing the water, and reading. When he was in high school, he and his buddies would come up to the lake with pilfered six packs. But now he just liked sitting at the edge of the sunlight reading a paperback, drinking Cokes, and listening to the radio from his truck.

Today felt different, though. He was tired. The caffeine made him jittery. He couldn't concentrate on his book and was fretting about the uneasiness at home. By noon, he packed up his chair and headed back to town. He thought about eating the sandwich Patti had made but set it aside for the factory-sealed bag of chips.

Ron-Allen waved as he passed Fred Gavus watering his lawn and was surprised to see a double handful of cars and trucks parked around the Tucker household. Two were in front of his open garage, and another two were across the street in Elise's driveway. Ron-Allen pulled up to the curb and went inside. The house was empty.

He tossed his keys on the kitchen counter, then headed out the door toward Elise's. He heard laughter from inside as he walked up her drive. He looked in the front window. There were a dozen women sitting around the living room. One, dressed in pink, was standing near the kitchen door. She was demonstrating something to the others. Ron-Allen couldn't see what it was, but the women enjoyed it. They animatedly passed it among themselves, talking and laughing. It was a sales party—kitchenware or makeup. Or, he smiled to himself, one of those housewife-sex-toy demonstrations he'd read about. No wonder Patti wanted to know how long he'd be gone.

Suddenly it was quiet. Someone had spotted him. He saw his wife get up from the couch. Too late to retreat. He met her at the door.

"Ron-Allen, what the hell you doin' here? You said you wouldn't be back until the middle of the afternoon." She looked up and down the street, then pulled him into the vestibule.

"Damn it," she said, almost in a whisper. "I'm tired of you sneakin' up on me."

"I'm not sneakin' up on you," he said. "I was just tryin' to find where you went."

A voice came from the living room. "Everything okay out there?"

"It will be," Patti answered. "He's alone."

Ron-Allen looked past Patti. Several of the women gathered behind her.

"If you're so anxious to see what we're doin'," Patti said, "why don't you just come inside?"

"That's okay," he said. "I'll meet you at home."

But Patti pulled him into the living room. He stood self-consciously in front of the women. None seemed glad to see him, except Elise, who sat on the couch and smiled.

The lady in pink reached down to the coffee table. "Try this one, Patti," she said. "It's our best seller." The women passed it across the room.

It was a beautiful, new handgun. Dull gray. Clean. Patti held it comfortably.

"And it has the new-member club discount," the woman added.

"I'll take it," Patti said and pointed it toward Ron-Allen.

He jumped back. The first shot went wide and missed him.

As the gun discharged, the women in the room leapt into action. Two quickly closed the drapes. Another turned on the stereo and jacked up the volume. A fourth rescued a fancy vase from an end table near him.

Ron-Allen stumbled backward into the front hall.

"I've had just about enough of you," Patti said and fired again. This time she nicked his shoulder. The pain was sharp but not debilitating. As Patti pulled the trigger a third time, he ducked. A mirror behind him shattered.

"Patti!" her sister yelled over the music. "Be careful. I just redecorated in there."

The gun jammed on the fourth shot. Two of the women came to help her, talking animatedly, checking the magazine, snapping it in and out. Ron-Allen sat stunned on the floor, holding his bleeding shoulder.

"The rug, the rug," he heard Elise shout. "It's new!"

In a flurry, one of the women pushed Ron-Allen sideways so he wouldn't bleed onto the carpet. Another set a towel on the floor to protect it.

Patti rapped the gun on the edge of the doorjamb. It fired unexpectedly, sending a bullet into the ceiling fixture. Startled, she lost her grip. The weapon hit the floor and fired again, taking the heel off a bystander's Italian leather import.

"Damn it!" Patti yelled as she picked up the gun. "Hold still, Ron-Allen."

She raised the weapon and sighted down her arm. Just as she was about to pull the trigger, there was a pounding on the door.

"Police! Open up!"

Ron-Allen used the distraction to roll out of Patti's line of fire. Her shot missed and lodged in the wall behind him. Before she could line up another, two deputies burst into the room and wrested the gun from her hand.

"One more! Just one more shot!" Patti yelled as they cuffed and dragged her out of the house. Before the door slammed, Ron-Allen caught a glimpse of Fred Gavus standing on the front step.

Someone shut off the stereo. The room was suddenly quiet. Ron-Allen sat up. His shoulder throbbed, but the bleeding had stopped.

One woman looked at him, then up to the ceiling. "Oh, Elise," she said. "It's a shame about the light."

"It's okay," Ron-Allen's sister-in-law said. "I didn't really like that one anyway."

In a moment, the women were talking and laughing as they cleaned up. A couple picked up empty glasses from the coffee table. Another vacuumed mirror shards out of the carpet. Elise had a can of spackle and was filling in the bullet hole in the wall behind him. Only one woman seemed to pay him any attention as he pulled himself to his feet. She picked up the towel on which he'd been lying and ran her hand over the carpet fibers checking for stains.

"You okay, Daddy?"

Ron-Allen looked up. Bobbi was standing next to him, munching on chips from a bag. "Yeah, honey, I'm okay." He put his hand on her head. "I didn't see you," he said. "Where were you?"

"Upstairs," she answered. "Playing video games with cousin Alison."

"Mr. Tucker?" It was the pink lady. "Will that be cash or charge?" she asked, all smiles, handing him a sales slip.

"For what?"

"That beautiful little widow maker your wife just bought." She pointed to the gun resting on the floor where it had been dropped. "I included Mrs. Tucker's new-member discount."

"I don't think she'll be needin' it," Ron-Allen said.

"But I can't take it back," the woman said, looking shocked. "It's been used."

Ron-Allen sighed. Reluctantly he reached for his wallet with his good arm. She wrote down his credit card number and handed him a receipt.

"I have a nice gift box for it," she volunteered. "It has a fitted foam insert."

Ron-Allen nodded. The woman picked up the gun, wiped it off, and placed it in the box. "I'll just add the five dollars to your account," she said as she put the box in a sunny yellow bag and handed it to him. "Y'all have a good rest of the day."

Ron-Allen and Bobbi headed across the street to their house.

Down the block, Fred Gavus was watering the flowers by his mailbox. Ron-Allen waved. "Thanks, Fred!" Ron-Allen shouted.

"No problem!" Fred shouted back. "Just being neighborly."

"I'm hungry, Daddy," Bobbi said.

"Me too. I haven't had lunch yet. Let me clean up and put this shirt in the laundry. I'll fix us a couple of sandwiches before I go and bail out your mom."

"Can I come? You promised."

"Not yet, honey. You're still a little too young," Ron-Allen said. "Maybe next time."

Digging Up Mr. Bradley
A Novel

AN EXCERPT

Chapter One

"I want to dig him up."

Alfred Williams Jr. leaned back in his chair and looked at the woman sitting in front of his desk. Mrs. Elsie Bradley was in her mid-sixties, but most would think she was at least five, even ten years younger. She took care of herself. She walked daily, exercised at a health club twice a week, and was meticulous about what she ate. She lived alone in a spacious co-op she had bought a dozen years earlier after her husband had dropped dead in the middle of a tennis game with one of his law partners.

"Can it be done?" she asked.

"Well, yes, it can be done," Mr. Williams Jr. said. "It's not that uncommon. Have you decided on a different plot?"

"No, I like the plot," she said. "I bought it twenty years ago. I like the view of the harbor. I want to be buried there. I want my kids and grandchildren to see the boats coming and going when they visit."

Mrs. Bradley liked Mr. Williams Jr. When Mr. Bradley died, Mr. Williams Jr. had been gracious, helping her through the process. And she had needed his help. Neither of her children would have been willing to step up to the task. She had expected that. Neither lived within a thousand miles of their New England home, and neither had ever liked Mr. Bradley. They thought it was a mistake for her to marry him and were barely civil to the man during the ten years he'd been their stepfather.

"Ma," Roger had said, "I'm glad you're happy, but I think you're rushing into this." It had made her smile at the time. She and Mr. Bradley had been seeing each other for well over a year.

Her daughter had been even less encouraging. "The man has no ethics," Christina had said. "Think about how he makes his money, representing criminals who should be in prison, getting them off. It's immoral. He's a sleazy bastard. I don't trust him and neither should you."

It was easy to dismiss their objections. Roger had been spending his college years as a film student working his way through a succession of undergraduate ladies unhappy in their majors and infatuated with bright lights. Christina was playing the rebel, majoring in literature, distrustful of authority, but volunteering for long-shot political candidates with no chance to change the world.

When Mrs. Bradley got the call from the hospital that fateful day of Mr. Bradley's heart attack, she had decided not to call the kids. It was a full two weeks before she wrote each of them a short letter saying that he was dead and buried. Roger called from California as soon as he'd received the news, asking if she wanted him to come home with or without his wife and kids. Christina wrote a carefully worded note acknowledging Mr. Bradley's passing and asking if her mother was going to burn his things, sell the house, and find a new place without his smell in it.

"So, then," said Mr. Williams Jr., "why do you want to disinter Mr. Bradley?"

"It's personal," Mrs. Bradley said.

"I see." Alfred Williams Jr. softly laid his pen on the desk in front of him and leaned back in his chair. "I'm afraid we do need to be a little more specific than that on the permit."

"Do most people put down a change of plot?" Mrs. Bradley asked.

"That is the most common," he answered. "But if you don't have another one in mind, what are you planning on doing with the remains? Cremation?"

"I haven't decided yet."

"But you have to decide," said Mr. Williams Jr. "We can't just dig up Mr. Bradley for no reason."

"Oh, there's a reason," said Mrs. Bradley.

"Excellent," said Mr. Williams Jr. leaning forward and picking up the pen.

Mrs. Bradley took a deep breath. "I recently discovered the slime bag had been sleeping with my daughter."

ॐ

Elsie Morad, nee Johnston, was in her early forties when Peter Joseph Bradley asked her to wed. She'd been married before, two decades earlier, for almost three years. Married to Scott Morad, a self-centered fellow who gave her two kids, a mortgage, and thousands of dollars in consumer debt before inconsiderately going missing in Vietnam a week into his tour. She'd been pregnant with Christina at the time, and not until after the baby celebrated her first birthday did Elsie Morad admit that her husband wasn't coming home. It was while standing in an A&P parking lot on a frozen Saturday morning in February. She was holding an infant in one arm, ignoring the tugs of a toddler on her skirt, and wrestling with the lock on her twelve-year-old station wagon. It was at that moment she realized two things: she had forgotten milk, and she was truly a widow.

Over the next ten years, she struggled to raise her children while working full time. It hadn't been easy. She had a job as a lab assistant at a university hospital. It didn't pay what she was worth, but it came with health coverage and free tuition for the courses she took to chip away at her undergraduate degree. By the time the kids were in middle school, she had finished her BS and started in a nursing program. By the time the kids were out of high school, Elsie had been on staff as an ER nurse for four years.

Both Roger and Christina went away to college, Roger to New York and Christina to Boston, and with an empty house, for the first time Elsie Morad did not feel the crush of life weighing her down.

She had met Mr. Bradley in the hospital when he was rushed into Emergency with chest pains. It turned out not to be life threatening, and he was released late the next day. But during the first hours as the doctors wired him up, poking and prodding for signs of doom, he had grasped Elsie's hand and held on believing she might be his last human touch.

The first summer seemed the sweetest. Mr. Bradley had a vacation house at the shore in Rhode Island less than two hours away. They spent a week there in July, sleeping late, walking the beach, and eating out every night. The kids visited the last weekend— Roger with some college girl, and Christina alone, morose, and carrying an anthology of the Romantic poets she was reading for a summer class.

"I was a lit major," Mr. Bradley had confessed during their Friday evening dinner. "Loved the Romantics."

Christina perked up when Mr. Bradley asked her if she'd read "Ozymandias" by Percy Bysshe Shelly. She had. She had also read the version written by Shelly's friend, Horace Smith, and published a month later under the same title. Throughout dessert, the two of them debated the significance of each, and why Shelly was the one still quoted—"Look on my works, ye Mighty, and despair!"

The discussion continued back at the beach house, Mr. Bradley and Christina holding forth in the family room long after everyone else had retired.

In the morning, Christina left abruptly before anyone was up with only a short note to Elsie that she had to get back to campus to study.

Over the rest of that summer, Christina had escaped to the beach house several times, alone, or so Elsie had thought. Elsie hadn't realized until years later that Christina's retreats coincided with Mr. Bradley's travel.

"I'm pregnant," Christina had confessed to Elsie over the winter break of her sophomore year.

Elsie had taken the news quietly but asked who the father was and if Christina wanted help making a decision about terminating the pregnancy.

"No one important," Christina answered to the first question. And, "It's too late," she answered to the second.

Although Elsie had given her the option to move home, Christina was determined to stay in school throughout that spring and gave birth to a daughter the week after finals. Elsie took a month off to stay with the new mom. By the end of summer, Christina knew she wouldn't be able to continue as a fulltime student but still wouldn't consider coming back home. Elsie helped her find a new apartment away from the campus and was grateful when Mr. Bradley arranged a job for her daughter with a former client. Two years later, without her degree, but with a chance to help her employer expand his business, Christina jumped at the chance to move to a different time zone and left with her daughter for Chicago before Elsie was able to visit one last time.

೪

It was a cold morning—sunny—but with a wind that came off the bay and swept up the hill through the stones. Mr. Williams Jr. had discouraged Mrs. Bradley from coming to the cemetery, but she had insisted. She wanted to make sure they opened the right grave.

When she arrived, the backhoe had already lifted away the sod. It was a methodical procedure. After digging down several feet, the men cleared the last of the dirt off the top of the vault and dou-ble-checked the identification fastened to the concrete. In a much shorter time than Mrs. Bradley expected, the casket was ready to slide into the back of the hearse. She had wanted Mr. Williams Jr. to open it then and there, but he was firm in his refusal.

Mrs. Bradley followed the hearse halfway back to the funeral home before turning into the parking lot of a big-box home cen-ter. She bought a plastic two-gallon pail that came with a snap-on top.

"Put the ashes in this," she told Mr. Williams Jr. when she stopped by his office a half hour later.

That evening, Mrs. Bradley sat on her balcony overlooking the park across the busy street. It had warmed throughout the day, and now the sun was setting behind the trees. She swirled the wine in her glass. On the table next to her, a portable cassette player sat amid a handful of tapes. Mr. Bradley had sporadically recorded his observations in an audio journal. After his death, she had discovered the tapes in a box of office miscellany rescued from his desk. It was months before she tried to listen to one. Hearing his voice alive and well spooked her, and she'd put the recordings aside. It was only recently, less than a month before, that she had rediscovered them in the back of her bedroom closet. Sitting in this same chair, she had pulled them out and listened to a couple. Some entries had been made while he was driving, but many were recorded in his office. She put her wine glass down and pushed the button.

"Next week I'll be fifty-five-years old," Mr. Bradley's voice said through the little speaker. "Fifty-five. Five five. The double nickel." There was a hesitation before he continued. "And life is still full of surprises."

Mrs. Bradley knew what came next. She had listened to this excerpt a dozen times. Mr. Bradley's phone rang. He fumbled with the recorder, thinking he'd shut it off, but he hadn't. And two decades afterward, between the pauses, Mrs. Bradley eavesdropped on one side of a distant conversation.

"I was hoping you'd call. You always leave so quickly . . ."

"You're right. It needs to stop . . ."

"She can't ever know . . ."

"I'll wait for you tonight at the beach house."

The sentence that came next was the one that had puzzled Mrs. Bradley the first time she heard it.

"Yes, she's your mother, but I'm not your father."

It had taken her a moment to process the statement and realize that he had been talking to Christina. It was a punch to the stomach that folded her in pain before she vomited over the balcony rail.

It had been almost two days before Mrs. Bradley was able to leave her apartment. She spent most of that first evening on the floor of her bathroom. The nausea was intense, and she barely had the strength to lift herself to the rim of the toilet each time it washed over her. By the morning, exhaustion had overtaken her and she slept fitfully for several hours on the floor next to her bed. When she woke, she was shaky but able to fix some toast and tea. She managed a shower, hands against the wall for balance. And she cried. Long sobs that made her fear she'd never be able to catch her breath.

By noon, she steeled herself to play the tape again.

"I was hoping you'd call. You always leave so quickly."

She wrote the seven sentences on a piece of paper and looked at them. She replayed them, listening to Mr. Bradley's tone of voice, picturing him at his desk. Was he anxious? Was he smiling? Was he glancing at the door, making sure no one could overhear? Was he leaning forward in his chair? Or sitting back? Was his heart racing? How many times had they been together?

"You always leave so quickly."

More than once. Twice? It had to have been more than twice. And they were going to meet again that evening. At least four times they would have driven the miles to the beach house. It was a two-hour drive from the Bradley home and equally distant from Christina's college apartment. Four hours total each way. Four times. Sixteen hours of anticipation. Sixteen hours of racing hearts, of breathlessness, and moist expectancy. When they met each time, were they tired from their drives? Did they put their keys on the kitchen table and sit for a drink? Did he hesitate before he touched her? Or did he grab for her as soon as the door had closed? Did he push her to the floor, groping and pulling at her clothing? Did she lie passive, or could she have been complicit, wrapping her legs around him? And where did they lie? Was it on the carpet by the fireplace? Or did they make it to the bed? Would Mrs. Bradley have smelled the coupling if she'd walked into the room that evening, or the next day, or the next weekend? Could she have found herself stretching across the bed unaware that someone familiar had marked over her territory?

For the rest of that day, Mrs. Bradley had parsed each of the sentences. She looked at the words. She listened to the inflection. She wondered how Christina addressed him. She imagined the missing sentences that filled out the conversation. She wrote them out and read them aloud.

She went back to old daybooks and cross-checked dates. There were four times that summer when Mr. Bradley's travel coincided with Christina's stay at the beach.

The second night after her discovery, Mrs. Bradley slept sporadically but felt rested enough to meet the sun. She drove to the cemetery and parked near the grave. She sat in her car for almost a half hour, looking beyond the monuments to the bay. A handful of trawlers and sports fishing boats crossed her horizon as they headed to open water. The sleeker ones moved slowly until they cleared the breakwater that marked the harbor entrance, then lifted themselves as they picked up speed.

It was chilly. Mrs. Bradley held the collar of her sweater as she walked among the stones. Mr. Bradley's was unadorned. It only had his name, date of birth, and date of death. There were no symbols of faith or icons of vocation. No pithy sayings or clever puns. Just the basics. The minimum. The simple facts of identity. Mrs. Bradley shook her head. Nothing is simple. Peter Joseph Bradley: attorney, husband, stepfather, father, sleazy bastard. The sixty-five years between the two dates were blank—unknown or forgotten or irrelevant. Except for the newly revealed secrets of that one summer.

"Fuck you," she said.

Nausea grabbed her and she threw up the little she had eaten that morning. It marked the granite face across the last letters of his name. She braced herself for a second wave but only coughed and spit. She wiped her lips with a tissue that she wadded up and dropped on the dirt.

The plot was a double, and the stone had room for a second name. Although she'd long planned on being buried here, she wouldn't be laid to rest next to him now. It was that morning she had decided to dig him up. Two weeks later, as she sat on her balcony listening again to his voice on the tape, she knew it had been the right decision.

Tomorrow she would pick up the ashes. And she would pack for a trip to Chicago to visit her daughter.

ACKNOWLEDGMENTS

I am indebted to a number of people for their support, advice, and patience, not only in pulling together this collection, but in the writing of each of the tales. To my friend, Howard Gross, who has been prodding me for years to assemble a collection of my stories, and to whom I finally said, "Okay . . . okay, enough already!" Thank you, Howard.

To Michele Orwin of Bacon Press Books for her guidance through the many decisions required to make this possible, and for her gentle reminders that although each story has to stand alone, when presented together, it's important to pay attention to how the themes, descriptions, and even the character names flow from one to another. To Lorraine Fico-White for her editing prowess, sharp eye, and willingness to let me make my case for keeping an odd word or awkward phrase before steering me back to a path that might be easier for the reader to follow. To Alan Pranke for his inventive cover design and to Lorie DeWorken for the interior design.

To Vivian Shipley, former editor of *Connecticut Review*, for her strong support of my work and her steadfast encouragement. To Jack Bedell, editor of *Louisiana Literature: A Review of Literature and the Humanities*, for his advice, guidance, conversations about writing, and willingness to share my work with others. To the late Susan Tavares-Tutt-Parsons and Bunny Tavares for their encouragement and support of my creative endeavors. To Rick Blum with whom I have shared many drafts of my work, and who always laughed, questioned, or grimaced appropriately. To Roberto Quiroga for his insightful questioning and philosophical discussions about character motivations, plot structure, and life in general. To Rich Lucas for his encouragement of my creative meanderings as we have worked together in various day jobs. To Muriel Levin who has been the first reader of many of these tales prior to their individual publication and who has provided valuable feedback and assurance, taking into consideration the occasional fragile confidence of the writer.

To my three boys, Justin, Alex, and Ben Tavares, who over the years seldom questioned why Dad locked himself away in the predawn hours to hammer away on his computer, making the assumption that everyone's dad did the same. To my wife Jennifer, whose patience with my ramblings about character or plot or word choice provided me the space and time to pursue those characters wherever they led.

I am also indebted to other friends, family members, and readers who have seen these stories in their previously published forms and have been kind enough to humor me with positive feedback. Finally, almost every day, I hear the voice of the late Leo Connellan, to whom this collection is dedicated, remind me in his gruff, no nonsense manner, "Writers write, Frank. Writers write." Thank you, Leo.

ABOUT THE AUTHOR

Frank Tavares has been writing his entire professional life but only began publishing fiction in the mid-2000s. His short stories have appeared in a variety of literary journals including *Louisiana Literature, Connecticut Review, Story Quarterly,* and *The GW Review.*

As a partner in a California ad agency, he gained a practical understanding of the power of words. Later, as an executive producer and a program head at National Public Radio, he learned to use that power for the forces of good. NPR listeners have heard his voice for years as the signature to all network news programs: "Support for NPR comes from NPR member stations and . . ."

Frank writes before daylight and in his day job, he is a professor of communication at Southern Connecticut State University. He is also one of the founding editors and active member of the editorial board of *The Journal of Radio and Audio Media.*

Made in the USA
Charleston, SC
07 September 2013